S0-ABB-874

JUNIOR LIFEGUARDS

Mayday

LB
X

JUNIOR LIFEGUARDS

BOOK
FIVE

Mayday

by

ELIZABETH DOYLE CAREY

DUNEMERE
Books

New York • San Francisco

PUBLISHED BY DUNEMERE BOOKS

Copyright © 2018 by Elizabeth Doyle Carey
Book and cover design by Jenny Kelly
Logo art by Jill De Haan
Cover image of coast guard by Eric Gevaert/Shutterstock.com

All rights reserved.
No part of this publication may be reproduced, distributed, or transmitted in any
form or by any means, including photocopying, recording, or other electronic
or mechanical methods, without the prior written permission of the publisher,
except in the case of brief quotations embodied in critical reviews and certain other
noncommercial uses permitted by copyright law.

Publisher's Cataloging-in-Publication Data
provided by Five Rainbows Cataloging Services
Names: Carey, Elizabeth Doyle, author. | Title: Mayday / Elizabeth Doyle Carey.
Description: New York : Dunemere Books, 2018. | Series: Junior lifeguards, bk. 5. |
Summary: Jenna Bowers and her friends must save a family from sinking when their
boat catches fire. Identifiers: ISBN 978-0-9988851-9-3 (pbk.)
Subjects: LCSH: Lifeguards—Juvenile fiction. | CYAC: Lifeguards—Fiction. |
Friendship—Fiction. | Heroes—Fiction. | Cape Cod (Mass.)—Fiction. | BISAC:
JUVENILE FICTION / General. | JUVENILE FICTION / Social Themes /
Friendship. Classification: LCC PZ7.C2123 May 2018 (print) |
LCC PZ7.C2123 (ebook) | DDC [Fic]—dc23.

The characters and events portrayed in this book are fictitious. Any similarity to
real persons, living or dead, is coincidental and not intended by the author.

ISBN: 978-0-9988851-9-3

J F CAR
1930 1129 08-16-2018 LJB
Carey, Elizabeth Doyle,

Mayday
    KHP

LeRoy Collins Leon County
Public Library System
200 West Park Avenue
Tallahassee, FL 32301

SPECIAL THANKS TO MODELS
LIZA SAUTTER AND HONEY HAMMAM!

JUNIOR LIFEGUARDS

Mayday

Ugh, I am SO TIRED of Samantha Frankel's bragging.

Today we were posted together out at Sea Spray Beach with Jamie, one of the town's senior lifeguards. Sea Spray is a busy ocean beach with lots of riptides and frequently big waves, and it demands a lot of attention from its guards.

But all Sam wanted to do was talk about all the celebrities she's met and all the fancy places she's been (most of which I've never even heard of), and the gourmet meals she's eaten, and the designer clothes she has. It's such a bragathon. Yuck!

Samantha is a rich and beautiful summer girl

who comes over from London to Cape Cod to stay in her seaside mansion each year, usually only for two weeks. But this year she's here for the whole summer *and* she's doing Junior Lifeguard training with me and my three best friends, so we've been forced to interact with her. She's also Selena's landlord and kind-of boss, or at least her parents (Somalian model turned newscaster Jemima Imari Frankel and Israeli billionaire David Frankel) are. Selena's parents run the Frankel estate and live on the property with Selena and her brother, Hugo, and their new kitten, Oscar.

As usual, Sam could not stop talking to me today.

"So, Jenna, at the dinner afterward—it was held at their palace on the coast—they released all these live butterflies to announce that dessert was being served on the cliff . . ."

"Uh-huh," I yawned. I didn't know who any of these people were that she was telling me about and I had tuned out when she was still describing the appetizers. I was sure Selena would kill to be hearing all this, being as celeb-obsessed as she was, but for me it was in one ear and out the other.

The water was rough today—not huge but a strong pull to the left, three-to-four-foot waves, rips everywhere. We'd had a storm yesterday, the day after Fourth of July, and the ocean had gotten really stirred up.

Earlier, Jamie had radioed in to Bud Slater, our head lifeguard, to ask about closing the beach to swimmers. But it was very warm and the sky was clear and—because it was the tail end of a holiday weekend—there were a ton of people on the beach. Bud said to give it an hour and we'd evaluate then.

We figured between me, Sam, and Jamie and the other senior guard, Steve, and his assistant, Kate, we could handle anything that came our way.

Technically, Junior Lifeguards aren't supposed to save people in danger. We're supposed to defer to the senior guards and watch and learn, like apprentices. But a few of the JLs had already had the opportunity to make a save and I was always hoping for a chance to shine like them. I wanted my turn to be singled out by Bud Slater at the end of the day so everyone could do the "three cheers" they always do for the guards who make saves, and then carry me to the water and toss me in, like always. And then the *Cape Cod Times* would do a small article on me, the way they usually do when a guard makes a good save. Even if it only made the online edition . . .

It was about more than the glory, of course. I wanted to save someone—to be a hero, the person who made a huge impact on someone's life, in a good way. And it was also about one simple fact: I *never* wanted anyone to drown. Especially not on *my* watch!

Now there were a bunch of younger boys in the water, probably around ten years old, riding the waves and hooting and hollering. We were observing them pretty carefully but then a little toddler girl wandered down to the water's edge without an adult and we took our attention off the boys for about forty-five seconds. I jumped down to grab her but Jamie got there first and swooped in just in the nick of time. A big wave was building and if it had hit the toddler, she would have been swamped and pulled under. I'd seen it happen a dozen times already over the summer: parents took their attention off a little kid for a minute and the kid got creamed by a wave. It was so scary because it can be hard to find little kids in the rushing whitewater aftermath of a wave, and most of the time, these kids couldn't even swim. I hated to see it.

My arms yearned for the muscle-pull feeling of a saved kid in them, and the joy and power of saving someone's life, but it was not to be. *Another day without a save for me*, I thought in frustration. *Another day without becoming a hero*. Yet as I climbed back onto the stand, Sam called out to us and pointed: one of the boys we'd been watching had been swept into a riptide and was being pulled quickly offshore to the deep water.

"Jenna! Cover! Get everyone out till I get back!" Jamie yelled at me, jumping down from our stand.

Her zillions of tiny brown braids slapped against her strong, dark shoulders as she ran into the water.

"Wait, let me come!" I cried.

"No! Stay and cover!" shouted Jamie over her shoulder as she ran to get the kayak. "And get everyone out!"

Steve jumped down from his stand and joined Jamie to help her. I wished it could have been me heading out there with her.

I blew the whistle for everyone to get out of the water. People looked a little panicky but Jamie was right—it was the best choice, since trainees weren't allowed to cover the beach without a senior guard.

Samantha and I stood on the lifeguard stand, watching helplessly as the strong current quickly pulled the boy offshore. It was so frustrating to just stand there and do nothing!

Jamie and Steve finally reached the boy and hauled him onto their kayak. His friends were clustered on the sand at the water's edge, their arms wrapped tightly around themselves, as a band of parents tried to get them to take towels. The boys waved them away, riveted to the drama out beyond the break. It was as if the boys wanted to suffer along with their friend until they were sure he was safe.

"I wish we were out there!" said Samantha, at my side.

"I know," I agreed, surprised she felt the same as I did.

We watched on in silence.

Soon Steve and Jamie had the boy aboard the kayak and were beginning to paddle back, but they didn't move. No matter how hard they paddled they just stayed in place. I could hear the anxiety building in the crowd on the sand below me: "What's happening?" "Why aren't they coming back?" "They're stuck!"

"They've got to get out of there!" said Samantha. "They need to try something else!"

Despite my confidence in Jamie and Steve, I was beginning to feel anxious, too. Their paddling wasn't a match for the strength of the riptide. Finally,

Jamie jumped out of the kayak. There was a gasp from below as people wondered what she was doing.

She went to the back of the kayak and began kicking, pushing it from behind as Steve paddled, and finally they were able to position themselves parallel to the beach and break out of the rip. You could almost see them propel outward as they got released from the whirlpool, and Jamie pulled herself back on board the kayak. They caught a wave and came skidding up onto the sand. The boy's parents fell upon him with a towel and hugs and then the dad turned to Steve and Jamie and began thanking them while the mom took the boy up to their beach setup.

Moments later, Jamie was back up on the stand with us, breathing heavily and toweling off. The water beaded off her muscles, and to me, she looked like a superhero.

"Wow!" I said. "Great job, Jamie!"

"Thanks," said Jamie, but she didn't look happy. "That shouldn't have happened. That was my bad.

The little girl distracted me and I should have been watching the boys while you dealt with her. Sloppy. Dangerous." She shook her head and sighed heavily as she wrapped her towel around her shoulders.

"I guess," I said. She was right. It shouldn't have happened. But she had handled it all really well. "At least you'll get the 'three cheers' today from Bud and then the dunking! I'm dying for that to happen to me one day."

"I've had it. It's great," bragged Samantha.

But Jamie gave a short bark of a laugh. "Yeah. Just what I need!"

"Don't you think it's fun?" I asked. "The dunking and everything?"

Jamie smiled, her teeth bright white and even. "I don't mind it. I just don't need all that celebration to tell me I've done my job. I mean, it's my *job*."

I thought about that for a second, and I knew she was right.

"But it's still nice," I said quietly.

Earlier in the summer I had quit swim team after seven years. I'd been traveling all over and competing at a really high level for a long time, but I'd lost my passion for it and my coach let me take some time off to try Junior Lifeguard training. It was fun to do something new and to have so much free time all of a sudden. But it was weird to never know how I was doing.

Swimming is all about stats: times, team rankings, town rankings, state rankings, and more. I was used to getting constant feedback on my performance, for better or for worse. I always knew where I stood. Now, even though I knew I was one of the better—if not the best—swimmer on Junior Lifeguards, I had no metrics; there was no way to measure myself against anyone else. Well, there were two ways, I guess, but I hadn't really experienced them yet. One was doing a save. If you saved a swimmer, you got the cheering and the dunking, and maybe a notice in the local news. But the other way to measure yourself as a junior guard was by how our director, Bud Slater, treated you.

Bud was stingy with his praise, though sometimes you could tell what he was thinking by what beach assignment he gave you for the day. Even though the senior guards have cautioned me not to read too much into it, I knew that when he was happy with something I'd done, he'd give me a sweeter position for the day—with a really accomplished senior guard on a busy ocean beach. But if he wasn't happy with me for some reason, he'd stick me at a baby beach up on the bay where nothing ever happened and the "senior" guards were amateurs.

I was grumpy after training today. I'd cheered along with the group for Jamie and Steve and watched them get tossed back in the water by the other guards. They handled it well, with Steve fake crying and fighting them off, and Jamie going rigid as a surfboard as they flipped her in feetfirst.

Plus Samantha had kept up a monologue the whole time about how she would have gone in for the save if they'd let her, and how she certainly would have gotten the boy out faster. I was so annoyed from listening to her all day that I thought blood would pour from my ears if she said one more word!

The afternoon had left me in a funk and as we walked up to our bikes, I knew my bestie Piper could tell. She's good like that.

"What's up, missy? Were you not impressed by Jamie's save today?" she teased gently. She let her bright blond hair out of its ponytail and shook it free.

I sighed. "I just wish it could have been me for a change." I can always tell Piper the truth, which is part of why she's such a great friend.

Piper flung her strong, tanned arm around me. "Missing the glory of swim team, are we? All those medals, standing on the podiums, people clapping . . ."

I laughed and ducked out of her grasp to face her. "How did you know?"

Piper laughed, too. "Jenna, come on! You're the most competitive person I know. I'm surprised you've gone this long without some kind of contest or competition."

"Oh no! Is it that obvious?" I cringed.

"Not in a bad way," said Piper. "Look, I get it: you're a strong swimmer, and you've been interested in being a lifeguard for a while now. I'm sure it's frustrating. It feels a little like Bud's holding you back. I can see that. But we're all still pretty green. There's a lot we don't know about technique and whatever, so it's not like he can just say, 'Okay, Jenna, you're a great swimmer. Now you're a senior guard.' You just have to be patient!"

I groaned. "It's going to take forever! I don't know how much longer I can wait before I see some action!" *And some glory*, I added silently.

"Look, just don't think about it, okay? You need to distract yourself from your craving for winning. Let's make a fun plan for this weekend. Something to look forward to. All four of us. Okay?"

Piper and I had reached the deck of the beach pavilion where our other two besties, Ziggy and Selena, were sitting waiting for us.

"Hey, girls!" called Selena. "Come!"

Selena was originally from Ecuador and she'd inherited her family's traditional dark hair, eyes, and complexion. She was simply beautiful—people on the street always checked her out—and her looks brought some buzz to our friend group. She and Ziggy were both petite, while Piper and I were tall and broad-shouldered and blond, raised from local farming and fishing stock: a little Irish/ Scottish, a little Polish, generally strong mutts.

We joined them at their weather-beaten wood table. "We need to make a super fun weekend plan," proclaimed Piper.

"Yesss!" said Ziggy. "Great idea! What should we do? Camp out at my house?"

Selena scoffed and rolled her eyes. "Backyard campouts are for babies," she said. "Nothing personal. What about bowling in Orleans? Or the drive-in movie in Wellfleet?"

"No, we need a real adventure!" said Piper.

I had an idea. I rolled it around in my mind for a minute, and then, feeling pretty sure of its appeal, I blurted it out. "Nantucket!"

"Totally!" said Piper, smacking her palms down hard on the table for emphasis.

"Ooh! I like that! Shopping, ice cream, celebrities . . ." said Selena. She was dying to be an actress one day and lived for star sightings (of which there are few in Cape Cod). Selena was convinced that all of Hollywood was out on the islands of Martha's Vineyard and Nantucket for the summer and she was missing out. We usually went once a summer, sometimes twice, and it was kind of our *thing*, as a group—a summer highlight and tradition.

"Ziggy?" I prodded.

Ziggy was thoughtful. "Would we go to Hyannis and take the ferry?"

"Well, it might be more fun if we could get my dad to take us. Then we could go out to Millie's for nachos in Madaket . . ."

My friends and I lived for Millie's. The food was awesome and the restaurant was set right on the beach, so it was fun and casual. Also, it was named after a kind of kooky old lady called Millie who was an unofficial Coast Guard back in the day. She was tough as nails and had saved lots of people from shipwrecks and sharks and stuff over the years. She was one of my idols.

"Yes, that would be *awesome*," said Piper. "Will we fish on the way?" Piper loved fishing and my dad loved having her on the boat because she's strong and such a hard worker. She grew up on a horse farm here in our town on Cape Cod, so she wasn't at all squeamish or scared of touching creatures.

"I'll ask," I said. "Probably, though. All in for fishing?"

"Sure," agreed Selena. "Can I film it for Facebook Live?" Everything was potential material for Selena's "brand" and her online image.

"Sure," I agreed. "Zigs?"

Ziggy was pulling at one of her springy black curls, lost in thought. Finally she scrunched up her small, fair, and freckled face and said, "Do I have to touch any fish, or watch them die or anything? Because that would bum me out big-time and also I don't think my mom would approve."

I pressed my lips into a thin line. Ziggy was an animal rights person—as were her parents—and I did not want to get into a whole debate with her about it. Obviously, with a fisherman for a dad, I came down on the side of humans in the fishing battle. "You don't have to watch, you don't have to touch, but you probably can't avoid smelling them."

"Also, does your dad use humane fishing practices? Maybe I'll go to the library today and email him a Best Practices guide from PETA, People for the Ethical Treatment of Animals, just so he's up to speed on all the new thinking about nets and stuff. That would make me feel more comfortable. What's his email address again?"

"OMG, Ziggy. That would *not* be a good idea." I could just picture my dad receiving an email from Ziggy telling him how to do a job he's been doing practically since he could walk, and his family for generations before that. "Just remember: freshly caught fish are organic and free-range, two of your favorite adjectives. And following proper industry guidelines, as my dad does, actually helps keep the fish stock balanced. Now, do you want to come to Nantucket with us or not?"

"I'd *love* to come!" trilled a voice behind me—female, with a British lilt.

Oh no!

I whirled around. "Uh . . . oh . . . hey, Samantha," I stuttered. "What's up?" I added lamely.

Samantha rambled, "Nantucket is the best! I have so many dear friends there, assuming their shows are on break from filming. There are all the places we always go to eat: Cru, The Pearl . . . and ooh, the Erica Wilson store! Nantucket is simply the best! And I couldn't help but hear you two discussing fishing. I absolutely adore fishing! We go halibut fishing in Norway each fall and fly-fishing in the Scottish highlands at Easter. I'm a dab hand at it, if I do say so myself . . ."

I nodded along lamely, feeling the situation spinning out of control. TBH, Samantha wasn't all bad, but she was sometimes rich-person clueless or even not-so-nice and it was awkward having her around. Somehow, though, she always managed to wiggle her way into our plans. And today I was so sick of her braggy monologue—I just wanted to get away from her.

My brain spun as I tried to think of a way to change the topic, but then Ziggy—spacey as always—said, "So what time would we leave for Nantucket on Saturday?"

"Uh, I . . ." I shot a dark look at Ziggy but she didn't pick up on it, and when I glanced back at Samantha, she was smiling so widely and happily, I just caved.

"In the morning," I said glumly. "Bright and early."

"I'm there!" said Samantha gleefully as Bud Slater walked by and called out his goodbyes to us.

"Oh, Mr. Slater, a moment of your time, please!" called Samantha, and she turned to catch up with him, calling to us over her shoulder, "Bye! Just let me know the details for the trip, okay?"

"You betcha!" said Piper, in a tone that sounded friendly but . . . wasn't.

My heart was heavy as I waved goodbye to

Samantha. I tried to focus on the nachos I was going to have at Millie's. They were worth any amount of hardship, I thought. Even having Samantha Frankel on board.

Little did I know just how hard the trip would turn out to be.

My dad was a commercial fisherman, which meant he fished on his boat for a living. If he wasn't out fishing (or more importantly, catching) every day, then we weren't getting new sneakers for school or a new roof or whatever it was we needed, big or small. *Sometimes* we could convince him to combine business and pleasure, and that's what I was hoping for when I approached him about taking us to Nantucket.

"Hey, how's the fishing out at Great Point Rip this summer?" I thought I was being pretty subtle, asking about the Nantucket fishing grounds, but he was onto me.

"Craving Millie's?" he asked with a grin.

I batted my eyes innocently. "What?" I stalled. I was clearing the dinner table at the time, so I acted busy.

He chuckled. "I know, I know. It's been a while. When did you want to go?"

"Oh, who, me? Nantucket?"

"Don't play innocent with me, kid. I could go for some fish tacos, myself."

"Saturday, please?" I blurted, placing the plates on the counter and throwing my arms around him in gratitude. "And can I bring my friends?"

"If they're willing to work. We'll fish Great Point first, then hit Millie's, okay?" He hugged me back and patted my head.

"Deal!" I agreed. "Can we go to town for an hour, too?"

"Sure. I'll go visit the cousins while you girls shop." My dad has cousins all over the place around here; most of them are fishermen and women, too.

We set the departure for early Saturday morning and I texted Piper and Selena to confirm. I'd tell

Ziggy and Samantha at Junior Lifeguards. Ziggy doesn't have a phone and Samantha—well, I didn't want to be too chummy with her. It seemed like too much texting would open a can of worms.

"Awesome!" replied Phoebe immediately.

"YAY!" typed Selena, in all caps.

Ziggy and Samantha were game for the trip when I told them at the beach the next afternoon, but we didn't have time to discuss it right away as Bud quickly called us all to order for news of the day.

"Guards," he said, after the boring logistic announcements were complete. "We've got a real treat planned for you this week. Thursday we're going to go see the Chatham Coast Guard fleet and meet one of their commanders. We've booked a school bus to bring us all over there and you can bring your lunch to eat on the short ride. It's a real privilege to get this kind of access and I hope you all can make it. We'll leave here promptly at noon, check out the fleet, meet a few people, learn a lot, then return. Back here by four o'clock."

"Yessss!" I said to my friends, pumping my fist in the air. This week was looking better and better.

"Glad to see your excitement, Ms. Bowers!" Bud called out. I blushed, hoping he knew my enthusiasm was genuine and not sarcastic.

I have always been interested in military service, and since I've always been a competitive swimmer, I figured Navy. But lately I'd been thinking about the Coast Guard. I was getting really interested in all this rescue stuff we were learning about as Junior Lifeguards, and I could definitely see making a life's work out of it. Meeting real Coast Guards and checking out their boats would be amazing.

But Ziggy was moping about it. "My mom will never let me go. You know how she feels about the military, plus there aren't any seat belts on school buses, and she gets all worked up about that . . ."

"Wait, do you *want* to go?" I asked. I wasn't dying to have anyone along who would harsh on my excitement.

"Ummm . . ." Ziggy smiled shamefully. "Not really?" she said, shrugging.

"Then don't go. I'm sure it's fine. It's not like it's required. It's just a treat. Don't you guys agree?" I asked Piper and Selena. They nodded.

"Totally," said Selena.

"Okay, phew!" said Ziggy, giddy with relief.

"I, for one, can't wait to go!" said Samantha. "I got to go to a christening of a new destroyer in the Queen's fleet last year. It was spectacular! All the airmen doing stunts and the marching bands playing, and the royals were all there . . ."

We all stared blankly at her, having nothing to add.

Finally I interjected, "Okay, but this is not going to be like that."

"Right. I know. Just saying." Samantha tossed her hair. "I'm going to get my towel," she said, and she strode off.

"Well, *don't* say," I muttered after her.

Ziggy's eyebrows were knit together in concern. "Hey, so what time do we set sail on Saturday?"

she asked, playing with a packet of free oyster crackers at the table.

"Well, for one thing, we're not sailing. My dad's boat is a forty-nine-foot Volvo commercial fishing boat with a 335 horsepower diesel engine motor, full Pullmaster boom winch, and Lobster hauler." I was feeling pretty broily now.

Ziggy waved her hand. "I know, I know. It's just a figure of speech. Chill."

"Early, right?" said Piper, squinting at me.

"Mmm-hmm." I wasn't dying to let them know how early we'd have to be up; I was worried they'd bail if they knew. Especially Ziggy. My dad likes to be on the water before the sun rises; as he always says, "Fish don't eat brunch." This means he usually leaves the house at four thirty in the morning.

Selena pulled her elastic from her hair, releasing her ponytail and shaking out her thick and glossy long brown hair. "I usually do my masks on Friday night. How early is early on Saturday?"

I cringed, and whispered, "Four thirty."

"Four thirty?! Are you crazy, chica?" Selena's

dark eyes flashed—the look she shot me was a cross of amusement and horror.

Ziggy froze in place, palms still in prayer position, mouth agape.

I smiled and shrugged, my own palms turned up in the air. "Sorry?" I said.

"Remind me why we like these nachos again?" asked Selena.

"You're still coming?" I asked hopefully.

"Of course." Selena redid her ponytail. "I'll endure any hardship for good food, and possible celebrities." Besides being an aspiring actress, Selena is an aspiring chef.

I laughed. "I'm not so sure about celebs, but we *all* know the food will be great. Zigs? You in?"

Ziggy sighed. "I guess, but it's going to be rough. I don't know if I can get my parents to agree to getting me there that early."

"Bett can pick you up on the way," offered Piper. Her grandmother Bett, who she lives with, is a super early riser. Most farm people are, by nature or necessity.

"Wait, I have a better idea! Why don't you all sleep over Friday night?" I said.

Piper brightened. She loves my house. "Great! Thanks!"

"Okay," agreed Selena. "Good idea. Can I bring my masks to your house?"

I waggled my eyebrows up and down. "Only if you bring them for all of us."

"Sweet," said Ziggy. "What about Sam?"

I stole a glance at Samantha, who was now flirting with one of the senior male lifeguards across the beach and cringed. She's so beautiful—with a mixed-race heritage that gave her incredible coloring, as well as thick and curly hair and huge green eyes and a long-limbed model's figure inherited from her mom. All the guys go crazy for her. "Ugh. Do I have to ask her?"

Selena quickly looked away. Whenever we have to socialize with Samantha, Selena just kind of checks out. It's super awkward for her to have Samantha around socially, at least in a group.

"I don't think it really matters," said Piper.

"Can't she have the manny drive her over on Saturday morning?"

Ziggy giggled at the word "manny," for "male nanny."

"Yeah, totally," I said. I couldn't begin to imagine Samantha at my shabby little house with all of us crammed in together: my parents, my three brothers, and then four friends, all in our three-bedroom house? No way. Not after what she's used to: yachts and mansions and five-star hotels. I got red-faced just picturing it. "Right, Selena?"

"Whatever you think," said Selena neutrally, rejoining the conversation. I knew Selena's mom had told her to try to include Samantha when possible. *Sam is very lonely*, said Mrs. Diaz, *and you're her only friends here.* This was a sad fact because we were really not very friendly at all.

But did she have to join everything?

On Thursday we all got to the beach early to make the bus to Chatham. I had a delicious packed lunch, courtesy of my mom's family's farm stand. They're known for their baked goods and prepared foods, as well as for the local produce, small-batch local packaged goods like honey, and freshly caught fish (thanks, Dad!) that they sell. Today I'd detoured over there on my bike ride to the beach and picked up some cornbread, coleslaw, sweet pickles, a salty piece of fried chicken breast, and a small jug of limeade. My aunt Suzie had tucked in a dozen freshly baked chocolate-chip cookies, still warm from the oven. She's famous for her cookies because she uses browned butter in them, which has a toasty caramel taste, plus she sprinkles a tiny bit of flaky sea salt on top of each cookie to enhance its salty-sweet contrast. I couldn't decide if I was more excited about my lunch or the field trip!

Piper peered into my sack of food when I got there and this time it was she who pumped her fist in the air.

"Go Suzie!" she said happily. "No one makes cookies as good as your aunt's. *No* one. Mmm. I can't wait!"

"What makes you think I'm sharing these, missy?" I joked.

"I'll mug you for them if you don't," she said, making a fist again.

"Okay! Down, girl! And quiet," I whispered, looking around and clutching my bag protectively. "We don't want to make the savages crazy or we'll have to share with everyone." Suzie's cookies were pretty famous in our town.

"Right!" agreed Piper, now keeping mum.

The bus ride was fun—all the boys were greedily peering over the seats to see what the girls had brought to eat, and I did end up sharing most of my cookies with Hayden Jones. He is super handsome but overly flirty with everyone, and kind of unreliable with a sketchy past (he got "asked to leave" his last boarding school). I go back and forth between liking him and avoiding him. Today I liked him, though, because he was joking a lot with me and was also really psyched about where we were going.

The bus drove down the hill toward the Chatham Fish Pier at the edge of town, and parked in the upper parking lot. We all disembarked and Selena immediately pinched her nose.

"Sheesh! It stinks!" she said.

The sun was blazing down on the parking lot and pier and heating up all traces of fish scales and fish guts left behind by the commercial fishermen of Chatham. It did smell pretty strong, even I had to admit it, and I'm used to the smell of fish.

But I poked Selena and said, "Get used to it, sister! This is what it's going to smell like on Saturday!"

"What's happening Saturday?" asked Hayden, who was walking down the hill toward the Coast Guard boats with us.

I exchanged a look with Selena; we'd already discussed the fact that Samantha was coming along uninvited. I didn't want to keep adding people. Plus having a boy along would change the dynamic.

"Oh, just a girls' trip to Nantucket!" I said lightly.

"Can I be a girl for the day?" joked Hayden.

"You make a better boy," said Selena, tickling him.

Grrr. Sometimes Selena really annoys me with

her instinctive flirting. It's as if she can't help it. She has to touch every boy and always joke with them and giggle, and it means nothing to her. It's totally not my way, and yes, maybe I'm a little envious of how good she is with them, all playful and light. But that's just not me.

It also irritates me because she knows I like Hayden as more than just a friend. But sometimes she says she likes him too and that makes me nuts. Anyway, for all of these complicated reasons, the last thing we needed was Hayden on our girls' day out.

"This way, kids!" Bud called, and we followed him down to the docks like a flock of baby seagulls and took a left.

Off to the right I spotted the local U.S. Fish and Wildlife inspector, Sidney Green—a.k.a. "Picky Sid"—the enemy of local fishermen. He hangs around the docks—all bald and chubby and blustery and always in a Madras plaid blazer, as if to set himself apart from the "dirty" fishermen and women—and boards the fishing boats as they come in. Then he checks their catch to make sure the fishermen aren't breaking any rules about size or haul limits. The fishermen respect the rules; after all, if the stocks weren't monitored, there'd be no fish left. But Sid was just so picky—he acted like he was out to get everyone, so they all hated him. I just avoided him when I saw him and today I was grateful to be heading toward the safe zone of the Coast Guard rather than the commercial fishing area. I'd much rather deal with rescues and military maneuvers than fishing cops with rulers.

Up ahead, tied up to the pilings, I could already see the silvery cabins of the Coast Guard boats winking in the midday sun. My pulse quickened. I've always loved military vessels: there's something about them that is so patriotic and brave and sharp looking. Coast Guard boats especially, since they're about saving people, not killing people.

There were about twenty of us in the group and we all clustered around Bud as one of the senior guards went to look for the mate who was meeting us for the tour.

Samantha yammered on to anyone who would listen about her glorious tour of the Queen's fleet; I wanted to puke and was glad when Bud started his little speech.

"Guards, I know many of you have seen the movie *The Finest Hours*, about the rescue of the crew of the tanker Pendleton when it broke up during a winter storm off Chatham in the 1950s. If you haven't seen the movie, go rent it at the video store . . ."

"What's a video?" called out one of the kids.

Bud smacked his forehead in frustration and shook his head. "Just watch it on your computer, or your watch, or whatever kids do these days to see movies. You won't regret it. It's a great film, all about the bravery of a small group of men—the rescuers and the ones who needed rescuing. Ah, here she is!"

She?

We turned to see a cute young woman with a thick blond ponytail walking quickly toward us. She was wearing a Coast Guard uniform: short-sleeved, dark blue cotton button-down shirt, and matching pants and made it look stylish. She grinned widely and waved hello as she crossed the dock toward us with the lifeguard who had gone to fetch her. I was ashamed of myself. I had automatically expected our Coast Guard officer to be a man—*me*, of all people!

"Hey, gang! I'm Kristen Healy," she said, shaking hands with Bud and the senior guard. "Come on along and see our vessels. I'll give you an overview of the Coast Guard and what we do. We love lifeguards around here, by the way. I started as a Junior Lifeguard myself, a long time ago, right Bud?"

Bud laughed. "Seems like five minutes ago to me, kid."

We followed her to the edge of the dock where the four boats were lined up.

"Lifeguards and Coast Guards share a lot in common," began Kristen. "In the Coast Guard, we have a motto: *Semper Paratus*, which means 'always ready.' I think it could be the motto for lifeguarding, too, don't you?"

We all nodded.

She smiled and continued. "And I have to say that lots of the lifeguarding skills I learned from this guy here"—she gestured at Bud—"are skills I still use in my job today. CPR, scanning the beach, looking after my gear, making water saves. It all started with Junior Lifeguarding."

Grrr! Again, I found myself wishing I had some water saves of my own.

"Now, we've got four boats of our own here in Chatham. There are three of these forty-two-foot Near Shore lifeboats, and then our new pride and joy—got it last summer—the twenty-four-foot Special Purpose Craft for shallow water. Come see!"

Kristen led us along the dock to where the boats bobbed gently in the harbor. A small, metal boat—almost like a dinghy or a Boston Whaler—was the first boat she showed us. Kristen patted the boat's stern. It had bright orange trim and two motors at the back that were tipped up way high out of the water.

"She's a beauty and we really needed her, because we kept running the larger boats aground. There are lots of shoals and sandbars around Chatham, as many of you probably know, and the waters—they look calm, but they can be risky." Kristen folded her arms and shook her head.

"We've got twenty-nine staff at the Coast Guard station up the road and we're a busy bunch. Especially during holidays like Memorial Day, the Fourth of July, and Labor Day, and also hurricane season. Visitors head out in boats they know nothing about, in unfamiliar water, and they get careless, maybe they're drinking, there could be some weather. Not good." She laughed. "Our new baby, this SPC, has a real shallow draft and she can take us right up on a beach if need be."

We walked farther along the dock to where three almost-identical, larger boats were tied up to cleats on the dock. They were in pristine condition, immaculately clean, with every bit of metal shining at a high polish and every rope tightly coiled.

"These other boats here are great farther out at sea. We call them the Arch Angels. They're self-righting, which means if they get flipped out in heavy seas, they pop back out of the water, right-side up. I'm sure a lot of you saw *The Finest Hours* movie, so you know about getting over the Chatham bar—the sandbar—and about beaching boats on shoals. But did you know some shoals come and go? With tides and waves, and weather, things move around, and if people aren't cautious, that's when accidents happen. Now climb aboard and see these beauties up close!"

Kristen let us all get on and check out every inch of the boats. Kids were opening and closing cabinets, doors, hatches; peeking inside the tiny cabins; asking Kristen questions; and chatting among themselves. I finally got up my nerve to ask her how she'd joined the Coast Guard.

"I went to the U.S. Coast Guard Academy in New London, Connecticut, for college—I always knew I wanted to do this. And then I came in straightaway. I was always inspired by the story of Madaket Millie, this woman—"

"Out on Nantucket!" I interrupted gleefully,

and Kristen grinned as I continued. "At the west end of the island, by Madaket beach!"

"Exactly!" she said.

"What a cool lady she was. Kind of a kook, but so dedicated, right?" I said. My favorite nacho restaurant was named after her!

Kristen nodded. "Her real name was Mildred Carpenter Jewett. She served in the Coast Guard auxiliary for decades and made lots of saves—starting when she was ten years old. They wouldn't let her actually join because she had bad eyesight. But after years of helping with shipwrecks and even some military stuff, she won our highest award for civilians and had a Coast Guard burial at sea."

"Cool," I said, sighing.

"Yep. So that's how I got into it. I wanted to train to become a rescue swimmer—there are only three hundred of them, kind of like Navy SEALs, and they get dropped out of helicopters at sea to perform rescues. It always looked so awesome. But I had to tap out of the training. I just wasn't a strong enough swimmer."

"Huh. I've never heard about that group." But the wheels were already turning in my head. When I was younger, I'd loved learning about Navy SEALs so much that I'd even named my cat SEAL. Maybe I should have a new life goal: rescue swimmer in the Coast Guard!

Suddenly a British-accented voice behind me piped up behind. "Must you be an American citizen to join? I'd quite like that for a job!"

My blood rose to an immediate boil. Samantha!

Luckily, just then, "Jenna!" called Piper. "Come!"

I managed to smile at Kristen despite my irritation at Sam. "You have a cool job. Thanks for all the info. I'm going to research that rescue swimmer thing online." I didn't want to leave but Samantha was standing there practically breathing down our necks and Piper was waiting for me on the deck of the other boat.

Kristen smiled back. "Great. Please feel free to be in touch if you have any questions. And hey, what's your name?"

"Jenna Bowers." I reached out my hand to give Kristen the firm handshake my dad always insists on. Then I thanked her and climbed off the boat to go find Piper. I left Samantha behind to tell Kristen all about the Royal British Navy and the celebrities she'd met while christening ships.

Piper and Selena were on the final boat—one of the forty-two-footer Arch Angels. Piper popped her head out of the cabin when I called her name. "Hey! I thought you'd gone and enlisted!" she teased.

"Ha-ha!" I said.

"Come inside. You'll love this!" she said.

I climbed aboard the boat and got behind the wheel, pretending to scout out a wreck or someone who needed saving, miming moving the wheel around efficiently. It was fun.

"Let me film you!" said Selena, whipping out her phone.

"Twenty degrees to north! Now correct five to south! Hold!" I said, mimicking emergency procedures I'd seen in videos on YouTube.

I looked over at Piper, a huge smile on my face, and she was shaking her head, laughing. "You're a goner!"

"It would be fun, wouldn't it?"

"For you, yes. For me, no way. I'm not brave enough," she said.

"I am," I said matter-of-factly. It was true. The ocean didn't scare me. People doing dumb things scared me. I definitely respected the sea, but I also knew you could learn protocols and skills to address any dangerous situation. "Plus, I do know my way around boats and how to read charts and avoid shoals and all that. I'm pretty good in the ocean overall."

Piper clapped her hand on my shoulder. "Jen, if I had to have anyone save me in the water, I'd want it to be you."

"Thanks!" I said with a smile. "Let's hope it never comes to that!"

"That's a wrap!" said Selena.

Friday afternoon, as I sat on the lifeguard stand at Sea Spray Beach and watched the heavy swell, I was distracted, thinking about my weekend plans. Luckily, I didn't have Samantha boasting in my ear today. My senior guard partner was Daniel, and he was good but quiet.

I was so excited for our sleepover and trip to Nantucket, I could hardly sit still. Saturday was predicted to have iffy weather—a possible thundershower, some choppy conditions on the water—but it would not dampen my spirits. I told everyone (even Samantha) to pack rain slickers and to bring flip-flops and a fleece for the trip. Rescheduling because of weather would be laughable in my family. The Bowers just push on and suffer. (Except for when it comes to food. We have pretty high standards for the quality and quantity of what we eat and the frequency of snacks and meals.)

My dad has a tradition of cooking a hearty breakfast on the boat, so he said he'd assemble the ingredients from the farm stand: biscuits, fresh eggs, locally cured bacon, and crumbly cheddar cheese from a dairy up the Cape. Selena's mom was going to make some arepas for us to bring along as snacks and tonight we were going to make some farm stand cinnamon buns to bring, too. My aunt Suzie had already sent over the dough, which needed to rise under a cloth on the counter before we assembled it into buns.

Selena planned to run home after lifeguarding to gather her face-mask ingredients for all of us, and Ziggy was bringing all this fortune-telling stuff she'd found at a thrift shop last weekend with her dad.

I love organizing, and I run a tight ship. I had mapped out our schedule for Friday night and all day Saturday, and made a list of shops we wanted to hit, scanning the Nantucket paper online to see if we could find any ads for stores having sales, or any coupons or anything. I wanted to get a new pair of flip-flops and stop by Vineyard Vines on the wharf. Selena's always up for jewelry or beauty products while Piper likes things to hold back her hair. Ziggy never buys anything.

I'd also planned out what to wear: warm sweats with a hoodie and raincoat for the boat ride and then a light, stylish cotton summer dress that I could change into when we got to Nantucket for our shopping and lunch.

I watched the passing boats and wondered if they were heading out to Nantucket, too.

Suddenly there was a shout, and I turned quickly to my right to see a little girl being crushed by a big wave. *Where is Daniel?* I looked around and couldn't see him anywhere. My stomach dropped. That little girl shouldn't have been out that far alone; I should have noticed and stopped her before it was too late!

I blew my whistle and gestured for everyone to get out of the water so I could make the save. But just as I was jumping down from the stand, a blur of red and brown shot by me, and it was Daniel. He pierced the water with a clean dive and disappeared underneath. Seconds later he shot up with a little girl in his arms, both of them gasping. People stood stock-still, including me, as he got her back to shore and made sure she could breathe.

Shame washed over me once I knew she was all right. How could I have let that happen? How had I not noticed Daniel was gone?

After a minute or two, he returned to our stand, dripping wet. I could tell he was ticked off at me.

He shook the water off his hair and mopped his face. "What's the deal? I asked you to keep an eye on things while I was in the bathroom, and you agreed. I only left for three minutes. You seem like you're really out to lunch today."

"I'm so sorry," I said quietly to him. I was embarrassed that I couldn't remember the exchange.

"You've got to have your head in this, Jenna. It's

mind over matter. If you feel your attention drifting, you need to drag it back. If it's not working, you have to go down a shift off the stand and just recover. Part of becoming a good guard is knowing this."

"Right. Okay. I know." I was mortified. "Are you going to tell Bud?" I whispered.

He took a deep breath. "I have to fill out an incident report about the save. If he asks me why I didn't avoid it, I'm going to have to tell him I was in the bathroom and I'd left someone else in charge."

My face flooded with warmth. "Okay," I whispered. "Right." I spent the rest of the afternoon laser-focused on every single person at the beach. I did not once let my mind slip. I knew Daniel had forgiven me once he cooled down, but I couldn't forgive myself.

Back at Lookout Beach at the end of the day, Daniel filled out his incident report and after Bud called for three cheers and the other guards went to toss Daniel in the water, Bud turned to read the sheet that Daniel had handed him. I was paralyzed, just waiting for Bud to call out my name.

Ziggy, Selena, and Piper chattered all around me, and Samantha was heading over to join our group, but I couldn't even hear what they were saying. My antennae were completely attuned to Bud. I saw his face darken and he lifted his head and scanned the group. Then he spotted me.

"Bowers!" he shouted, but my feet were already moving me toward him as the blush spread up my neck and face.

"Sir?" I said meekly as I reached him.

"What happened out there today at Sea Spray?" He folded his arms, the incident report in one hand, flapping in the shore breeze. His eyes were steely blue, awaiting my reply.

"I was not on . . . I didn't . . . I did a bad job," I said lamely.

He kept looking at me, waiting for me to elaborate.

"I . . . uh . . . I didn't realize Daniel had left. I mean, he told me he was leaving, but I was distracted, and uh . . ." I didn't want to get Daniel in any kind of trouble. Obviously it wasn't his fault I hadn't listened to him or noticed he'd left.

"Yes? And?" prodded Bud.

"I didn't realize I was on. Like, that it was all on me. And I just didn't see the little girl go out so far."

Bud stood looking at me, his lips a thin line. "Miss Bowers. If I impart one lesson to you juniors this summer, let it be this: lifeguards are always 'on.' There is no *off*. Just like what Kristen said about the Coast Guard the other day. *Semper Paratus*: Always ready. Do you understand? There's no time for bad days, or distraction, or thinking about something else, no matter how important. Do you understand?"

I nodded miserably. "Yes, sir. I'm so sorry."

"There's no room for sorry when it comes to life or death. You don't need to apologize to me. I'm just glad you don't have to apologize to that little girl's mother for her drowning on your watch." At that, Bud turned on his heel and strode away.

Tears of shame and frustration pricked at the

corners of my eyes. I wanted so badly to cry but I absolutely wouldn't. I raised my eyebrows and breathed through my mouth, tipping my eyes to the sky to roll the tears back into their ducts. Luckily, most of the guards were down by the water still dunking Daniel, and my friends were up behind me.

Once I'd collected myself, I took a deep breath and turned to climb the dune up to the pavilion to rejoin my friends and start my weekend. My excitement was muted now. I was upset and embarrassed and most of all, mad at myself for being careless.

Samantha came bounding over, all enthusiasm, her long dark mass of curls bouncing behind her. "So I'll meet you at the Chatham Fish Pier tomorrow at four thirty, then?"

I snapped out of my daze and regarded her in surprise. "Oh. Yes. Great." I cringed inside; it suddenly seemed awful of me to not invite her to sleep over. But now I just couldn't. If I was going to lick my lifeguarding wounds tonight, I couldn't add her in, too. She'd had a save and two assists already this summer and was the darling of the program and a favorite of Bud's, despite a bit of a rocky start.

"Fabulous. I'll bring something for the ride, too. I can't wait to show everyone all my favorite places! Maybe we'll see some of my dear friends—"

"Thanks, Samantha," I said, cutting her off. I did not need this now: her taking over my fun plan, my tradition with my friends, all on top of my horrible day today.

Her smile faded. "Okay. See you." She started to walk away but then she turned back. "Sorry you missed another save today," she whispered warmly, like a confidant. "See you tomorrow. Ta-ta!" And she took off.

Aaargh! Why had I agreed to let her come in the first place?

Selena, Piper, and Ziggy were bouncing in excitement when I reached them, and they all began talking to me at once.

" . . . at six thirty . . ."

"So we need to wash it off after twelve minutes exactly . . ."

"And *extra* frosting this time . . ."

"Okay!" I said sharply, and they all clammed up simultaneously, giving me strange looks.

"What's up?" asked Piper.

"Are you not psyched anymore?" asked Selena.

I sighed heavily and explained what had happened earlier, leaving out the Samantha part.

Piper looked at me with a stricken expression. "Yikes. That's scary. Thank goodness the little girl was okay. Sorry for you, though—I know how badly you want to do well with this."

"Thanks, but it was totally my fault."

Ziggy waved her hand. "Don't take it all too seriously. We're just trainees."

I swallowed my rage at that comment and decided not to reply. Ziggy was barely interested in lifeguarding; she was only doing Junior Lifeguards because it allowed her full-time access to the beach and its creatures—the Piping Plover birds she protected, the wildlife fish tanks she'd set up, and the garbage pickup and recycling she liked to do.

"It's a pity this had to happen on a Friday. Now

it will ruin your weekend because you'll be stewing about it for two whole days," said Selena.

I nodded. "Yeah. But I deserve it."

"Jen, stop. You're the most conscientious Junior Lifeguard there is. Don't beat yourself up. Everyone makes mistakes. It's normal." Piper was trying to be supportive, I knew, but it didn't help.

I shook my head. "Not for me," I said. "I'm heading home. I'll take a shower and try to shake it off. I'm psyched to see you guys in a bit, okay?"

I'd already deflated their happy moods. There was no need for me to ruin their weekend, too.

"Okay. Fun times ahead!" sang Selena.

"Woo-hoo!" cried Piper, high-fiving Ziggy.

I went to get my bike from the rack as they all chatted further. Suddenly Bud was by my side again. I gasped. I hadn't seen him coming.

"Your head really is in the clouds today!" He smiled. "Listen, I was harsh back there intentionally. I wanted to shock you a bit, shake you up. But I don't want this to upset you. Every day is a learning experience, especially when you're a junior. I'm still learning things myself. You've got good things ahead of you, kid. Keep your wits about you and keep on trying, all right?"

I nodded. "Thanks. Yes. I'm sorry."

Bud patted my head. "Buck up. See you Monday."

I climbed on my bike and pedaled home, feeling that my dream of "three cheers" and being thrown in the water was farther away than ever.

By six fifteen, I felt a tiny bit better. I'd showered and organized my room for the sleepover and my gear for the Nantucket trip. I'd been online again and searched to see if there were any lingering Fourth of July sales at the stores I liked there. I'd updated my list of places I wanted to hit (Monelle's, Salt, Milly & Grace, Stephanie's, Shift), and did a small checklist of the ice cream stores in town so we could debate over which one to go to after Millie's—they each had their advantages. (Even Millie's Market ice cream had its advantages!)

At 6:29 Piper arrived, with Selena right after her. Ziggy didn't roll in until nearly seven, when we had already started eating dinner. Some of my little cousins were over, as was usual on Fridays. My mom's family farm stand's biggest day of the week is Saturday, so her sisters do a lot of prep work and cooking on Friday nights. My mom's job is to host all their random kids for dinner while the moms are at work. It makes for crazy Fridays and often times I'll just lock myself in my room to avoid them all, but this week with my friends there, there was no escaping it. My mom made a huge batch of chicken tacos with all the fixings (also a Friday-night staple) and kids tore in and out through the sliding doors while my friends and I sat in the living room with plates balanced on our laps.

"Sorry about all the chaos," I said for the millionth time.

"I love it. It reminds me of being at my *abuela*'s when we were still in Ecuador," said Selena from the floor, lounging back against the bottom of the sofa.

"You're lucky you have all this family," said

Piper. She was living with her grandma while her dad started a new life with a new family in Pennsylvania and her mom worked off-Cape at a big job opportunity in Ohio.

"Yeah, and they're all here in Westham!" added Ziggy.

Piper and Selena and I exchanged glances. Ziggy had family here in Westham, too, but she didn't know it. One day soon we'd have to get to the bottom of the whole Bloom family mystery, but not tonight.

"Little kids are awesome," said Selena. She only has her older brother, Hugo, and Ziggy and Piper are only children, but Piper and Selena both babysit, as do I. Junior lifeguarding has us around kids all afternoon, every weekday, too.

Just then, my three little cousins came tearing through the room. My twin little brothers, Finn and Gavin, were chasing them and the dog. They raced out to the fort in the backyard and my friends and I all looked at each other and started laughing.

"How awesome are they now?" I joked.

"I'm going to have lots of kids one day," said Piper.

"Not me," said Selena. "I'm going to be famous."

"Hey! Perfect timing! Let's do the fortune-telling!" said Ziggy.

We quickly picked up our plates and helped my mom clean up the kitchen. With all of us helping, it was done in a snap, then we headed to my room to find out what the "future" held in store for us. I didn't buy into this sort of thing but it was Ziggy's contribution to the sleepover, so I was going along with it.

Ziggy insisted on turning out all the lights except this tiny book light that I usually clip to my loft bed so I can read at night. She opened her patchwork bag and started removing objects—cards, a crystal ball on a stand, a bag of something jingly.

"Ziggy! This is the real deal!" said Piper.

Ziggy nodded. "Shh. Now we must be solemn as I get set up. Then we will invite the energy into the room with some chanting and incense."

"I can't have anything lit in my bedroom. It's a

family rule," I said. My dad is paranoid about fire.

"Okay, then I will spray some essential sage oil to purify the space instead," said Ziggy in this weird trancelike voice.

Piper giggled. "Do you just carry that stuff around?"

"Shh!" droned Ziggy, closing her eyes. "Be in the moment."

Selena and I grinned at each other. Ziggy was totally making this stuff up as she went along.

Ziggy felt around in her tote and came up with a spray bottle that she spritzed around and kind of on us.

"Smells good," I said, sniffing the air.

Then Ziggy started chanting. It sounded like nonsense to me. "Omnia konichiwa. Eeny meeny desolini, ooh-aah ahbolini. Achi kachi kumerachi . . ."

The other three of us were about to die laughing but we went along with it and after our laugh attack subsided, there was nothing to do but let Ziggy carry on. Finally she said, "All right. Who wants to go first?"

Selena chimed in, "Piper. Let's see how many babies she's going to have."

Ziggy nodded, her eyes still closed. She waved her hand over the crystal ball and hummed. Then she said, "Come spirits. Tell us the future. What is in store for Piper Janssens?" She kept waving her hands and then she began to talk.

"Four little boys, three are yours, on an island, animals. Many animals. A big man. Handsome. Dark skin. Lots of hair. Fabric. Lots and lots of fabric." She lifted her head and opened her eyes. "Ooh. That was weird."

Now we were all somber. It had seemed really real for a second, what Ziggy was saying.

"It was like a picture appeared and all I had to do was describe it."

"Do me! Do me!" begged Selena.

"Okay, rune stones or tarot cards or the crystal ball again?" asked Ziggy, offering her wares with a flick of her hand.

"Do the same thing you did for Piper."

Ziggy closed her eyes again and began to hum.

"Come back to me spirits and tell me. What do you see for Selena Diaz in her future?"

We leaned in toward Ziggy, not wanting to miss a word. The room felt warm and snug.

Ziggy began to speak.

"Flowers. Bright red flowers. Red satin dress, red shoes, lights. A stage. A man in a suit. Music and laughter. Pearls on a string." Her head snapped up and she looked at us all wide-eyed. "Cool! That was really cool!"

Selena's arms were wrapped around herself as if for warmth. "Is there more? Were there crowds? Money?"

Ziggy shrugged. "I don't know. I didn't go that far into it."

"I think I'm definitely a performer of some sort, right?"

"Definitely," I said with a firm nod. "And if there are flowers, you're definitely a star."

Selena gave a satisfied nod. "That's what I thought, too."

"Jenna? You want me to do you?" asked Ziggy.

I waffled for a minute. I usually don't go in for this sort of stuff but it was kind of cool and fun what she'd said about the other two. I shrugged. "Okay? I guess?"

Ziggy nodded, closed her eyes, and started doing the hand waving over the crystal ball again. She hummed and called the spirits and quickly began to talk. "Water . . . boats . . . boys . . ."

Selena and Piper and I exchanged smiles. All of this was to be expected. Ziggy was obviously just telling each of us what we wanted to hear.

But then she gasped. "Fire! Sirens! Sinking!" She snapped her eyes open and stared wildly at us, then lunged to turn on the floor lamp next to my beanbag. Ziggy was breathing heavily, in a panicky way.

"Ziggy! Don't leave me hanging! What the heck was all that about?" I demanded. "And what happened next?"

Ziggy looked scared. "I . . . I don't know. That was really scary and weird. Sorry." She shivered visibly. "Whoo! That's enough for one night. Let's go watch some TV!" She jumbled all the fortune stuff back into her bag and stood. The other three of us just sat there on my rug, dumbfounded. Ziggy doesn't even like TV.

"You're just going to leave it like that?" I asked.

"Yup," said Ziggy briskly.

"O-kaaaaay . . ." I said. I was kind of ticked.

Selena and Piper spoke at the exact same time.

"Cinnamon buns!" and "Mask time!" and the moment was broken.

By the time the cinnamon buns had baked, filling the whole house with the mingled aromas of cinnamon, browning butter, and caramelizing sugar, we were well finished with our face masks; our faces were squeaky-clean, smooth, and hydrated.

We each laid out our clothes for the next morning, along with our outerwear and other accessories, and a small tote bag each for hauling home any purchases. Because we were getting up at four fifteen, we needed to just automate everything.

Selena's mom's arepas were tightly packed in a small cooler, my dad had his breakfast sandwich fixings in his cooler, and my mom promised to wrap the cinnamon buns for us once *they* had cooled.

My friends and I turned in at nine thirty—a preposterous bedtime for a sleepover! But with our early wakeup call, this get-together was really about tomorrow and not tonight.

As I snuggled into my sleeping bag on my floor (we'd done a coin toss for my bed and Piper had won), my emotions swirled. I thought back with a cringe to my near miss today at the beach, with anger about Sam's comments, and then moved on to fear with Ziggy's creepy predictions.

Fire?

Sirens?

Sinking?

"**M**ake it stop!" cried Piper from my loft bed.

My phone alarm was chiming us awake. It was already five minutes after four. My adrenaline kicked right in and I was alert and ready. I stood and pulled on my clothes. Piper clambered down the ladder and went to use the bathroom. I turned on the overhead light and Selena pulled the covers over her head; at least she was awake. Ziggy hadn't even budged. She was out cold.

By the time we'd all dressed and gathered our things, my dad was waiting in the truck with the top off his steaming thermos of coffee.

We'd loaded all of our stuff in and then at the

last second I remembered the cinnamon buns and had to dash back to get them.

No one spoke as we drove to the dock. The truck rumbled through the darkness, the heater on low even on this July morning, the aroma of coffee hanging warm in the air. There was a light mist and the truck's wipers went *whump* every fifteen seconds or so to clear the windshield.

Selena rested her head against the cool window in the back but her eyes were still open. Piper was bright-eyed and eager in the middle seat. I was wide-awake but Ziggy had already dozed back to sleep. Over to the pier and down to the dock we cruised, then into my dad's usual spot against the parking lot's stockade fence. Like zombies we exited the truck, gathered our things, and trudged after my dad.

"Where's Samantha?" asked Piper, looking all around. There were a few other pickups parked in the lot—fishermen, for sure, who'd already gone out—but no shiny Range Rover.

I shrugged. "I'm sure she'll be here any second."

Once we reached my dad's boat (the *Kerry Marie*, after my mom) and loaded on our gear, he went in to start things up and ready some of the fishing gear. I stowed the cinnamon buns in a safe spot in the galley, stashed the arepas in the fridge, and instructed my friends where to tuck their things in the cabin. I showed them the tiny bathroom and the cooler of drinks, and then I announced that I was going back to meet Samantha.

"Five minutes, honey!" called my dad. "Sun's coming up!"

I turned my head; he was right. The dark blackness of the night sky was lightening up just slightly. It was hard to tell, what with the cloud cover, but it would soon be dawn.

I jogged back over to the parking lot and looked up the hill. I pulled out my phone. Nothing. I wondered if I should text Samantha, or even call her.

I folded my arms, a little shivery from the early wake-up and the misty weather. I jogged in place for a minute. Then I texted Samantha: *You up?*

I looked at the time. My dad is a psycho about

punctuality. I had about two minutes grace period left; Sam was already eight minutes late. She was never late for Junior Lifeguards. My skin tingled with nervousness. Where was she?

Fire? Sirens?

Ziggy's weird predictions and chanting flashed though my head. But no. If something had happened at the Frankels' we certainly would have heard. Selena's mom would have called or texted her. I was feeling really guilty now that I hadn't just said what the heck and asked Samantha to sleep over, too. It had been mean of me.

I tapped my toe and noticed that I could see my breath coming out in fluffy white plumes. I sighed heavily out loud and refreshed my screen. Still nothing.

Sam?

I typed again and pressed send. No reply. Cringing, I pushed the phone icon to dial her and it went right to voicemail. So she wasn't even up yet; that figured. She'd probably been up late, partying with celebs or something. We were just small potatoes to her, a backup plan. I should have known.

I turned in annoyance and headed back to the boat, picturing Samantha lying in a giant bed with pink silk sheets and a pink satin eye mask over her eyes. I had to admit: I was glad she might not be coming.

One thing I love about my dad's boat is the sound system. He had a really good year two years ago and he gave into a craving he'd had for a long time and bought a sick stereo system. This morning he let us hook Selena's phone up to it and she DJed as my dad pulled us out of the harbor. He wouldn't let us turn up the volume until we were well offshore and moving at a good speed, but for now it was nice to have a cool soundtrack as we headed out.

"So do you think the princess just overslept?" asked Piper.

I sighed. "I don't know. She's always so eager to be with us. I doubt she would miss it."

Ziggy nodded. "It's weird that her phone is off."

"I'll text my mom in a little bit to have her go check," said Selena. "Let me give it until five thirty. I don't want to wake my mom any earlier than she already gets up."

I checked my phone again after about six minutes of put-putting through the harbor at low speed. We were almost at the mouth of the harbor and there'd be no turning back after that.

Finally there was a new text. My fingers scrambled over the screen to get to it; I dreaded having to ask my dad to turn back. In fact, he'd most likely say no.

But Samantha wasn't asking for that.

Transportation problems, her text said. That was all.

I showed it to the others.

"Maybe her Ferrari wouldn't start?" said Ziggy with a wicked smile.

I went over to the console in the wheelhouse to talk to my dad.

"What's up, angel?" he asked.

I told him about Samantha's weird text and he sighed. "Do you want me to go back?" He looked pointedly at his watch and then at the sky. "I'd like to get ahead of that weather that's supposed to skim through here midday."

I got the hint. "No. That's okay."

I typed back: *R u ok? We had to leave. So sorry. Will make it up to u.*

My finger hovered over the send button and then I just pushed it. There wasn't anything I could do at this point. We were nearing the mouth of the harbor. A boat passed us coming in and we all waved.

"Okay? Ready?" asked my dad.

"Ready. Hold on to something, girls!" I called.

Everyone grabbed a handle or plopped into a seat and as we passed through the opening in the barrier island, my dad pushed the throttle all the way up while simultaneously reaching for the volume dial on the stereo.

Katy Perry blared across the open ocean and all my friends screamed and cheered. The mist was turning into a fine rain now and with the spray from the water kicking up, all of our hair was soon soaked. But we were dry inside our raincoats and we sang along with the music at the top of our lungs as we roared away from the land and toward Nantucket waters.

After about twenty minutes of all-out flying across the water, my dad killed the engines and we bobbed in place for a bit as he prepared breakfast for us in the tiny galley kitchen. I sat in the high, padded captain's seat and steered the boat into the swells as they rolled in, as directed by my dad. There weren't too many other boats out today—it was foggy, chilly, and still early. We saw three fishing boats and two ferries, but no pleasure craft at all.

Ziggy was starting to look a little queasy.

"Pipester, get Ziggy a Coke from inside, please. Full-sugar!" I ordered, like I was the captain myself.

"Oh, I'm not allowed to drink Coke . . ." Ziggy protested weakly.

"Ziggy! Get a grip. It's medicinal," said Selena as Piper returned and cracked open the cold red can.

"Drink," said Piper.

Ziggy stared at the Coke can like it held poison, then she reluctantly took it and managed a small sip. She looked at us and took another small sip. Then she grinned and took a huge swig and we all laughed.

"See?" said Selena.

Ziggy took another huge gulp, did a massive burp, then turned and threw up over the side of the boat.

"Oh, dear," I said. The smell of the diesel fuel and the up and down of the waves can be really hard on some people out here. Plus the fog made the horizon invisible and without a horizon to get your bearings, it could make anyone feel a little loopy. Why didn't it surprise me that Ziggy was today's victim?

I checked my phone again and there was another new message from Samantha. It said:

Sorted. Where r u now? Will come meet.

What? Was she planning on meeting us out
here? How?

"Uh, Dad?"

I stepped down from the chair and with my
hand on the wheel, leaned into the galley. The
smell of bacon hit me hard and I was starving all of
a sudden.

"Yum!" I said, and the boat took a major wave
broadside and lurched.

"Jenna! Steer into the waves!" barked my dad.

"Sorry!" I grabbed Piper and told her what to
do, then I ducked into the galley. "Need help?" I
asked.

My dad shook his head. "All set. How's Ziggy?"

"She'll live. Listen. If Samantha wanted to catch
up with us, what should I tell her directions-wise?"

"Why doesn't she just meet us in Nantucket
around eleven if she's got a ride?" asked my dad.

I shrugged. "Should I tell her to do that?"

"Yes. We'll meet her at the wharf. Rory will drive us out to Millie's and join us for an early lunch. Then you girls can hit town while I check out his new rig. Breakfast in two minutes."

Rory is one of my dad's favorite cousins, also a fisherman.

I typed back to Samantha:

Meet us at Nantucket Wharf? 11 AM.

Moments later my dad was handing out bacon, egg, and cheddar sandwiches on homemade biscuits, each wrapped snugly in this drip-proof waxed paper pocket he makes, like an origami hat upside down.

There were cries of happiness as my friends bit into them. Even Ziggy managed a few bites of her bacon-free one before she fed the fish again over the side of the boat.

My dad's radio crackled. There was a bunch of chatter but I couldn't really hear it over the music. My dad leaned in. He and all his buddies chatted on the radio during the day, covering fishing conditions and weather tips, shooting the breeze, teasing each other. They spoke in a weird jargon I didn't understand, so I basically never paid attention.

"Cut the music, kids!" barked my dad suddenly.

I jumped to unplug the phone from the system, and then it was crazy silent, except for the gusts of wind and the splash of the ocean. The radio flared again with a burst of chatter.

"What's up, Dad?" I asked when it had died down again.

He pressed his lips together into a thin line. "Sounds like something or someone's gone aground on Lucas Shoal, by the Vineyard. Shh. Listen."

He tipped his head to the radio as a bunch of voices started talking. My friends and I looked at each other with raised eyebrows. I still couldn't make out what they were saying. But then I heard one thing loud and clear: *Coast Guard*.

"Yikes," I whispered, grabbing a fighting chair as the boat bucked against a wave unexpectedly. "It's got to be serious if the Coast Guard's going in."

My dad started doing all sorts of stuff to the

radio and talking to people as we finished up our sandwiches and cleaned up the pans in the galley.

When everything was neat and stowed, I returned to my dad at the wheel. I just stood, not saying anything as he listened to the radio. Finally he turned to me.

"A ferry ran aground on the shoal. Darndest thing. No one knows these waters better than the ferry drivers. Crazy things happening in the waters these days. Gotta be global warming." He shook his head.

"Is anyone hurt?" I asked nervously.

"Nah." He stood. "They don't need us. They've got every available boat for thirty miles heading in to help. Let's hit the Great Point Rip while we have it all to ourselves. Steady, girls! Let's go catching!" he called. Then he pushed the throttle and we roared off toward Nantucket.

5

The *Kerry Marie* bobbed in the water off the top of Nantucket point. The Great Point Rip is fertile ground for striped bass and black sea bass at this time of year. We were trawling, which means running with the lines in the water. Ziggy had taken a Dramamine motion sickness pill and gone to take a nap in the cabin. Piper had already hauled in two huge stripers and Selena was also totally into it, which kind of surprised me. I did not think of her as the fishing type, but it was all fodder for her Facebook Live and her other social media accounts. She was blathering on about movies now, like *The Finest Hour*, *Titanic*, and *The Perfect Storm*—films

I preferred *not* to think about while on the open ocean.

After a bit, my dad cut the engine and we hung in the water, lines stretching out on both sides of the boat. We hadn't seen any other boats except the scheduled Nantucket ferries since we'd set out, which was very unusual. My dad had been monitoring the grounding of the Martha's Vineyard ferry on the radio. It seemed they'd have to wait until high tide for it to lift off the shoal, but no one was hurt and they thought the boat would be fixable. All of his fishing boat friends had gone to see if they could help (or really just to see it for themselves, I'm sure), so they were reporting back to him by radio and mobile phone.

I hadn't heard from Samantha again. I assumed she'd meet us as planned, at the wharf at eleven o'clock. I prayed it wouldn't be raining out there then, because Nantucket in heavy rain is a bummer.

"I've got one! Fish on! Fish on!" Selena was squealing. "Film me!"

My dad laughed and came to stand by her side.

"Easy now. Okay, let your line run a little. Tire him out. Easy . . ."

Piper grabbed Selena's phone and filmed while Selena struggled with her fish.

I could hear the far-off whine of a very powerful high-speed boat engine. At first I didn't pay it any attention, but it was so quiet out that I finally had to turn and see what it was.

Off in the distance I could see a boat, its prow high out of the sea, displacing a ton of water as it raced toward us.

"Dad! Check it out! Is that a cigarette boat?" Cigarette boats are high-speed racing boats. They're very pricey and they're not something you see often around Cape Cod. They're more of a Hamptons boat, or Miami Beach.

My dad turned and looked. "Yep. Coming in hot, too." Hot means fast, in boat-speak.

He turned back to check on Selena's fish and when he was satisfied that she was holding fast, he came back over to my side, scooping up his binoculars on the way.

He trained his binoculars on the boat in the distance and looked through. "For sure he sees us, but he's heading right at us. Idiot. He's gonna scare the fish away." My dad sighed heavily in annoyance and put down the binoculars to fiddle with the lights on his wheelhouse. I grabbed the binoculars and peered through the lenses. I could see a guy driving the boat as they drew closer.

"What the heck is that?" asked Piper, who had joined me at my side of the boat, Selena's phone held limply at her side.

"A little help here, please!" cried Selena. My dad rejoined her but Piper and I stood watching the cigarette boat.

"Do you think they're going to hit us?" asked Piper, her forehead wrinkling.

I passed her the binoculars and she lifted them to her eyes. "No, he sees us."

Piper passed me the binoculars back with a wry smile. "Look again," she said.

I lifted them to my eyes again. As I focused on the rapidly approaching boat I could see another figure beside the captain, leaning over the side and waving her arms. She was in a yellow slicker with the hood up but her long dark curls spilled out of the sides of the hood, uncontainable.

"Samantha!" I said in surprise.

I looked at Piper, who was grinning at me. "Where there's a will, there's a way, that's what Bett always says."

I laughed. "My grandparents say that, too."

"That must've cost a pretty penny . . ." said Piper as the cigarette boat downshifted and started to draw alongside us. The noise of the engine drowned out the rest of what Piper was saying and anyway, I put my hands over my ears to block it out. Finally the guy cut the engine and drifted up next to the *Kerry Marie*.

"Ahoy! Ahoy!" cried Samantha, waving her arms like crazy.

We waved back. I was friendlier than usual, trying to make up for the non-invite to the sleepover and the departure without her this morning, as annoying as she was.

My dad and the other guy threw ropes across and hauled the boats together. Then the cigarette boat guy dropped a plank across the two boats and Samantha quickly scampered across.

Once onboard the *Kerry Marie*, she hugged us all (Selena had to one-arm it, because she was holding her rod), then she waved and blew kisses to the captain of the other boat, calling, "*Ciao,* Ramón! *Besos, mi amor!*" Ramón turned and roared off, spraying a huge plume of water out of the back of his boat in a giant arc. We all laughed. It was like something out of a Kardashian show.

I introduced Samantha to my dad, who was totally confused by her. She is not my usual type of friend. But to her credit, she said, "Mr. Bowers, how can I help? Please put me to work. I'm good on boats and I've fished a lot."

My dad shot me an impressed look and set Sam to cutting some bait fish while he helped Selena begin to reel. Her fish was tough and did not seem to be tiring. My dad went to turn on the boat to drag the fish for a bit. The mist had drenched all of our hair and it was cool out but sticky from the dampness: really bad soupy weather.

"So what happened this morning?" I asked Samantha.

"Ugh. Not worth even discussing." She gave her head a shake and tossed the chopped fish in a bucket at her feet. I couldn't believe she wasn't even wincing at the aroma; I'm *used* to fish guts and I still hate the smell.

"Okaaaay . . ." I said. "We felt bad."

"Please don't," she said briskly. "How's the fishing today?"

Piper and Selena and I filled her in on the day's haul so far. We'd done decently, but my dad wanted to move a little further offshore to the northwest for a bit, then we'd loop back down and right into the harbor to meet Rory for the ride to lunch.

For now, he cut the engine again to help Selena finish reeling in her fish. Selena had Piper disconnect her phone from the stereo system and film her for Facebook Live as she reeled it in. It was a good-sized fish with a lot of fight in it. Once it was in the boat, my dad handed the huge creature to Selena to pose for Piper. It was a black sea bass—really long—more than half as tall as Selena! My dad unhooked it and it flapped around on deck for a few seconds until my dad dropped it down into the hold (thank goodness Ziggy slept through all that). Selena was so proud! She filmed some more footage for Facebook, then reconnected her phone to the stereo and cranked up the tunes.

Samantha wanted a turn in a chair with a reel next, so my dad set her up and she hooked a huge fish almost immediately.

"Hey!" said Piper, joking. "You just got here! How'd you hook one so fast?"

Samantha tossed her hair. "Loads of practice!" she said, which made me hate her again a little.

Sam's fish took a while to get in; Selena played a whole playlist of fight songs at top volume during the battle. Once Samantha finally reeled it to the side of the boat we all scurried to look over the side as my dad netted it and lifted it on board.

The boat lurched and Piper lost her balance and nearly pitched over the side.

"Whoa!" she cried.

"Steady!" said my dad, nearly dropping the fish as he reached for Piper. But Samantha grabbed her in time and Piper smiled nervously. "Sorry. All good."

"Nice save," I said to Samantha. "We might have to do three cheers and then you know what comes next . . ."

"Uh-uh! No way! Not out here!"

I waggled my eyebrows at her. "Tempting!" I said, pretending to push her to the side of the boat.

She squealed and my dad hushed us suddenly as he lifted Samatha's giant striped bass out of the net.

"Sorry," said Samantha meekly. It was weird for me to see her subservient to someone else for a change. I kind of liked it.

But my dad wasn't hushing us because we were bugging him. "There it is again. Kill the music!" he said sharply.

"Dad! What is it?" I put my hand on his arm.

"Take the fish," he said, thrusting it at Samantha. He skidded over to his radio and turned the volume way up.

It crackled and we all stood stock-still, listening.

And there it was. "Mayday! Mayday! This is the *Free Spirit*. Help! Five souls on board!"

My dad clicked through his radio and spoke into his receiver. "I hear your Mayday, *Free Spirit*. This is the *Kerry Marie*. Do you copy?"

He looked at us without seeing us, his eyebrows knit together in deep concern. My friends and I looked at each other in alarm.

"Mayday! Yes, I hear you, *Kerry Marie*. Oh, thank God! Thank God!"

Now my dad raised his eyebrows. "Where are you, *Free Spirit*? What's happening? Over."

"We're . . . uh . . ." There was the sound of shuffling around and the radio crackled in and out.

Samantha gripped my arm hard. "Oh my goodness," she breathed quietly.

I had chills all of a sudden. The wind was

picking up and the rain that had stopped was re-appearing as a fine mist again. Waves smacked the side of our boat but I hardly noticed anymore.

"*Dad!*" I whispered urgently.

He held his hand up to silence me. "*Free Spirit*, this is the *Kerry Marie*. Do you copy?"

The radio crackled. Then we heard the guy. "*Kerry Marie*, this is the *Free Spirit*. We're off the backside of Chatham. We've run aground on something. The dashboard is sparking. We've got kids on board. Three kids. Two adults. Oh my God. Help, please, help!"

But my dad was already flipping switches on his console, reeling in the trawling lines with the automated winches, all of the mechanicals humming and squealing as they pulled.

"Secure everything. Get inside!" ordered my dad as he spun the wheel with one hand to change our direction 180 degrees. He continued to hold the radio receiver in his other hand.

My dad barked into the receiver, "Sit tight, *Free Spirit*. We're not too far. We're coming to get you!

Over." He continued on shouting into the radio, communicating with the Coast Guard and all his other friends, telling them about the *Free Spirit* and our plan to find them as we zoomed back toward the Cape.

My friends and I scrambled down into the cabin and onto the daybed there, pushing the dead-weight of Ziggy aside. She slept on, totally clueless, as we wiggled in and braced ourselves with our backs against the wall. The engines roared and as my dad pushed it full-throttle, the prow of our boat lifted way up and we fell back toward each other, scrambling to stay upright, kind of laughing but also knowing nothing was really funny right now.

"OMG, you guys," I said quietly, my eyes huge.

"This is so scary!" said Selena, hugging herself in her raincoat.

"Thank goodness Ziggy's sleeping through all this drama," said Piper, looking down at Ziggy.

Samantha reached over and unfolded a fleece blanket, draping it over Ziggy's shoulders. *Hmm,* I thought, watching her unexpected kindness.

"Never mind the drama; thank goodness she slept through all the fishing!" I said with a smile, and we all laughed a little.

"What happened to you this morning?" Piper asked Samantha. I tried to give her the side-eye to drop the subject but Piper didn't notice, so I sighed and waited for Sam to avoid the question again. But this time she didn't.

"Nigel happened. Or rather, Nigel didn't happen. Please don't tell your mum, Selena!" said Samantha desperately. Nigel was the manny.

"Tell her what?" asked Selena.

Samantha sighed heavily. "He had some friends in the area last night and they went out clubbing in P-town . . . he rolled in at around three thirty and he was in no shape to drive me down to the dock. I couldn't even budge him at four. He was out cold in his bed."

Selena pressed her lips together and shook her head. "That's really not fair."

"Not fair?! It's downright dangerous!" said Piper indignantly. "He could do something that gets you all killed, like leave the stove gas on or something!"

Samantha cringed a little. "He *is* a liability. But when he's good, he's really good, I swear. He's fun and he lets us do whatever we want—not in an irresponsible way; just, he helps facilitate fun stuff. I'd really hate to have some ghastly proper nanny in a uniform looking after us, and that's what's coming next. A real battle-ax." Samantha shivered. "I'd just hate it," she added softly.

There was an awkward pause as we all digested this information. I suddenly felt an unfamiliar pang of sympathy for Sam that she had to deal with all this. Though it seemed glamorous, her life wasn't all fun and games. There was no question that her actual parents might come and look after her; it went without saying that they would not. They had major jobs (though from Googling them, they also seemed to have major social schedules, too. They were always in photos with royalty and celebrities, dressed up in ball gowns and tuxedos). They just didn't have time to come all the way over here to Podunk little Cape Cod.

After the silence, Selena spoke first. "I really do think my mom should know. At the very least for safety purposes, you know? And my mom really likes you and Alessandra . . . She'd go crazy if something happened to you. And she can't stand Nigel!"

"She must know he's wild," said Piper.

Samantha sighed and shrugged. "Let's leave it for now, okay?"

"For now," said Selena. She lifted herself up a little on her fists to see if she could get a look out of one of the rectangular porthole windows along the wall. But she collapsed back down glumly. "I can't see anything. I'm too short."

I glanced through the windows on the other side of the boat, but I didn't really even need to look. "There's nothing to see out there. Trust me. Just water and more water."

"Maybe I should heat up the cinnamon buns," said Piper. She'd been eyeing them all morning.

I smiled. "Go for it. But you're in charge of them. Keep an eye on them, okay?"

"Got it." She scurried off the bed and lined up

the buns on the little tray of the toaster over, then powered it on. She turned to us and smiled. "We could all use a little sugar."

"Oh, Samantha! I forgot my manners. Would you like a snack or a drink?" I offered.

"Sure . . . thanks . . ."

But right then my dad leaned his head down. "Jenna! I need you. Come up here!"

My friends and I exchanged anxious looks. "Selena, will you feed Samantha, please?"

I cringed as I climbed back up to the deck. I wished I hadn't just asked Selena to basically serve Sam. Selena always feels touchy about her status around Samantha. But when I reached the deck and peeked back down, Samantha was helping herself to a Coke and an arepa, and I relaxed a bit.

"Are we close?" I asked my dad.

"Very. But now that we're close to land we've got some bad fog," he said. "I need your eyes. I'm taking the engine way down to a crawl. You use the spotlight and see if you can help me find the *Free Spirit*. I want to check a shoal I know about.

I betcha that's where they are. If not, I just don't want to hit it myself, okay?"

"Got it." I scrambled up to the front of the boat and switched on Dad's huge spotlight. Sometimes he uses it for night fishing, or to unload a catch in the dark. Today it was . . . well. I didn't want to think about what it was for.

"*Free Spirit*, we're close. Do you read me? Over." My dad spoke into the radio.

Suddenly something really awful pricked at my nose. "Dad! What's that smell?" I cried.

"Burning plastic," he said. "Burning boat," he added quietly, but I heard him. "We must be close."

Suddenly a chill washed over me.

Fire. Sirens.

OMG.

Sinking.

6

"**D**ad, what about the Coast Guard?" I said urgently. "What about them helping? Should you call them again?"

My dad shook his head. "The call is in but they're all tied up over Martha's Vineyard way with that ferry. If it's bad, they might scramble out a helo, but the rescue boats are too far gone."

A helicopter? I gulped.

"Keep moving that light around out there, Jen!" he called. I slid it from side to side and up and down, doing arcs and lines. "And don't worry. The guard knows we've got the *Free Spirit*. We're good. Let's just find these guys now."

"Hello! Hello!" I called urgently as we cruised silently through the thick fog. "Hello! Hello!"

Wait! I thought I heard something.

"Dad!"

"Shh! I heard it, too!" He got on the radio. "*Free Spirit*, this is the *Kerry Marie*. We think we're close. Shout if you can hear me." He cut the radio and engine and we listened. I could actually feel my ears moving on my head as they pricked up, attuning to any possible sound.

"Help! Mayday! Help!"

I whipped my head around to look at my dad. "It sounded like it was coming from over there!" I pointed to my left and my dad nodded and re-started the engine, gently turning the wheel a bit to the left.

"Hello! Hello!" I continued to call.

"Help! Help! Over here!" Their calls were getting louder as the smell of burning plastic got even more acrid. I pinched my nostrils shut with my free hand.

"Whoa!" called my dad as he cut the engine and backspun the wheel. The *Free Spirit* was suddenly right next to us and we had to back away a bit to avoid hitting it. My dad threw our boat into reverse and our engines roared and strained at the gear change, like wild diesel animals.

"Oh thank God!" a woman's voice called. I lowered my light to point down onto the water so it wouldn't blind anyone.

"*Free Spirit*! We're here!" called my dad.

"*Kerry Marie*?" called a man's voice.

"The one and only!" said my dad.

Their boat was sitting high at a really weird angle. It looked like a child's drawing of a boat, with the boat completely out of the water and all the waves smacking its sides below. Except that it looked like it was about to tip over. My dad pulled away to circle the boat and the woman on board became a little hysterical.

"Wait! Don't go away! Where are you going?" she cried in a panic.

"Helen, calm down right now!" said the man sharply. I didn't blame him for being mad. Her cries were terrifying me!

"I just want to see where I should pull up to take you on," said my dad calmly. "Don't worry. You've got a little bit of time still."

The woman started wailing again and I heard a kid say, "Mom! Stop!" in a pleading voice.

The back side of the boat was even scarier because now I could see where the smoke was coming from in the console. I heard my dad's sharp intake of breath as he saw the smoke. He sprung right into action.

"Okay, let's get you all off there right now. Quick, quick!" He said it in a friendly tone but I could tell he was really scared all of a sudden. I think "Helen" was right to be in a panic, judging from the urgency in my dad's voice.

"We've got the boys!" wailed Helen.

"It's all right. We'll get you all. Don't worry. Now I need you to listen to me . . ."

As my dad issued instructions, my friends peered up from the cabin. Ziggy was up now— whether they'd woken her or the Dramamine had worn off, I couldn't be sure—but all of my friends' faces were horrified.

"Stay there!" I scream-whispered to them, and they all nodded.

My dad had circled back around to the other side of the boat, where he could get closer. He cleated a rope onto our boat and flung it over to the *Free Spirit*, where the man caught it. "Pull us in close, but not all the way," instructed my dad. "Jenna, be our buffer. Girls, come help!"

My friends scrambled up out of the cabin, their faces rigid with fear. We all exchanged silent looks as they held out their arms to ward us off from hitting the other boat.

"We've got to make this quick," said my dad. "Give me the kids first!" I knew my dad was telling the truth about not wanting to get stuck, but I actually thought he was worried that their boat might explode. I was sure worried.

A little boy of about five years old appeared at the top edge of their boat, his father's hands holding him at the waist from below. The kid's face was a mask of terror and he was crying.

"Hey, it's okay, buddy. Come on. You're going

to be fine," said Samantha, reaching out to him. The rest of us stayed as buffers while she grabbed him and helped him down on our deck. "Stay right here by me, and hang on to my raincoat. What's your name, big guy?"

He was speechless, gripping her raincoat with white knuckles, so she patted him on the head and cooed, "Don't worry. It's all going to be just fine. Next!"

The next boy looked just like the first but he was around eight or nine.

"Okay, big guy. You can do this," said Samantha encouragingly.

"Jenna, grab the wheel!" barked my dad as he dashed across to help Sam lower the boy onto our deck.

"What's your name?" asked Samantha.

"Jack," he said. "And that's Freddy." He jerked his thumb at his little brother.

Samantha passed her hand over Freddy's head again. "It's okay, Freddy," she said gently. "It's going to be just fine. Stay by me."

"He's shivering," said Piper.

"Here," I called from the wheelhouse. I took off my raincoat and hoodie and flung them at Piper. She draped one over Jack's shoulders and the other over Freddy's. Now I was bare-armed in a T-shirt over my bathing suit but I barely felt the cold, I was so revved up on adrenaline.

"Okay, here's our injured guy!" called the dad from the *Free Spirit*.

"Is he bigger than you?" I called over to Jack. He nodded.

Then Jack said, "His name's Michael. He has a broken leg."

I snapped my head up and looked at him. "What?"

"He's on crutches," said Jack somberly. "He can't walk very well right now."

"Piper!" I shouted. "Take the wheel. Keep it pointed due south!" She nodded and slipped into the captain's seat.

"Dad!" I whispered, rushing to his side. "This guy's—"

The older boy appeared at the top of the other boat, his face even more terrified than the others. He was *very* good-looking, about my age, and he was clearly scared but not crying like the other brothers. His hands gripped the rail of his boat and he didn't seem to want to let go.

"Come on, big man," said my dad. "We've got you."

I could see the other dad's arms shaking as they struggled to hold the injured boy up in the air to hoist him over the side. The boy struggled to push himself up and over.

Suddenly, with a big push, he came up and over the rail . . . and dropped straight down into the water.

"Michael!" shrieked the mom.

"Oh my . . . !"

In a flash, I kicked off my flip-flops and clambered up on the gunwale of our boat, then I flipped a leg over the side and dropped in after him.

The water was freezing and I gasped as the shock of it hit me. My T-shirt and sweats were soaked; they dragged me down in an instant. The waves were hectic and breaking every which way. As my head popped above the surface, I searched for Michael. I spotted him about ten feet off to the side of me, kind of floating in place. Everyone above me on the boats was shrieking but I tuned them out.

"Michael!" I called.

He didn't turn.

With great effort, I paddled over to him.

"Michael!"

He lifted his head and looked at me in a daze. There was blood streaming down his face. It looked like he had a big gash over his left eyebrow.

"Michael! We've got to get you on the boat!"

He seemed to come alive a little, and began clawing at the surface of the water, looking around. Just then a life preserver ring attached to a rope dropped into the water beside me.

"Jenna!" shouted my dad. "Quick!"

I grabbed the ring and pulled the last two strokes over to Michael.

"Michael. Listen to me," I said, making eye

contact and following the procedures Bud had taught us. The words flowed naturally right out of my mouth. "I'm a lifeguard. I'm here to help you. You have to listen to me, okay?"

Michael just stared at me. He was in shock, I could tell.

"Michael!" howled his mother from the boat. "Michael!"

I pulled the ring to him and put his hands on it. "Hold on tight. I'm going to come behind you and push."

With great effort, against the slapping waves, I pulled behind him and started to push him back toward the *Kerry Marie*. I kicked with all my might, but I was moving against the tide or the current and it was like I was swimming in place. It reminded me of Jamie trying to save the boy from the riptide with the kayak the other day. I slightly changed my direction to see if I could break free of the current. The water was in my eyes but I couldn't let go to wipe them clear, and my hair was all over the place, plastered to my face.

"Come on, Michael!" I encouraged. "Let's go!"

I tried not to think of his blood dripping into the water and the new migration pattern of the great white sharks who liked to summer off Chatham these days. I just kicked with all my might and prayed, but no luck.

Suddenly there was a splash in the water next to me and Samantha surfaced. She was wearing a hot-pink bikini (bikinis are forbidden in Junior Lifeguards, so some people wear them like crazy when we're off-duty) and her hair was back in a new ponytail.

"Sam!" I spluttered in surprise.

"I got this," she said, diving down under the water and pushing Michael up from below. Quickly they were at the side of the boat, while I lamely paddled after them.

My dad had pulled a winch on a boom over the back of the boat and he carefully lowered the hook down to us in the water. This is what he usually does when he hooks a big tuna.

"Jenna! Hook the life ring onto the winch.

Samantha and the boy, you two hold on and I'll pull you up!" he commanded. "Jenna, swim to the tailgate after and we'll let you up."

I took a deep breath and grasped at the huge iron hook as it came down to the water level. My hands were so cold and I was shaking so badly that it took a couple of tries to loop the ring onto the hook.

"Hurry!" barked my dad.

Michael's mom was wailing and his dad was praying out loud. I finally got the rope through and the hook snapped shut over it. I looked up at my dad—his face was ashen and his eyes were wide with fear. I gave him a quick thumbs-up sign with one hand and he nodded back at me, one quick jerk of the head.

Sam wrapped her arms around Michael. "Go!" she shouted to my dad.

"No, put him in the preserver and you hold on!" he shouted back.

Sam looped the ring over Michael's head and maneuvered it under his arms so he was hanging in it, then she grabbed on to it as well. The winch began to lift them.

The grinding metal-on-metal noise of the winch made it sound like it would break and drop them at any minute. As they lifted out of the water and hung above the waves for a moment, Samantha clutched Michael and his broken leg stood out at an odd angle in its cast. I closed my eyes and stroked over to the tailgate of the boat, my arms shaking with the effort. It was only seconds before the tailgate lowered. Piper's arms reached out to grab me, and then there were more hands—Ziggy's—pulling me aboard. I collapsed in a heap on the deck of the *Kerry Marie* but my friends turned away to help the others once I was safely aboard. Thank goodness, or they would have seen my tears and fallen all over me. But my tears were not tears of relief; they were tears of anger and frustration. How had I failed to complete a save, yet again?

I shook my head, going over the events of the previous few minutes and wondering why Samantha had jumped in. Why had she been able to get

Michael moving and up and out of the water, while I hadn't been able to? Was I the worst lifeguard who'd ever lived? Quite possibly.

"Piper! I need your help!" barked my dad.

Piper quickly pivoted to the side of the boat and helped my dad grab the mom, Helen, from the *Free Spirit*. Helen fell onto our deck and then rushed to Michael's side as her other boys joined her—all of them clasped into a giant hug, weeping and gasping.

Now it was time to get the dad over. He had gathered their things and was handing bags and Michael's crutches over to my dad. The smoke from the *Free Spirit* was now a steady black plume.

"Okay, forget the rest of that stuff, now. You've just got to get over here. We need to get away *now*!" commanded my dad.

The other dad understood. He perched on the side of their boat and pushed off, grabbing my dad's hand and launching himself onto our boat. At that, my dad shouted, "Push off, girls!" and Ziggy and Selena gave the *Free Spirit* a huge shove while my dad dove over to our console and gunned our engine, spinning the wheel to get us away.

Mere seconds after we'd peeled off from the *Free Spirit*, there was a huge *boom!* and the entire console of their boat burst into flames.

"Oh my God!" shouted Helen.

The father covered his face with his hands. I think he was crying and didn't want us to see.

"Dad!" cried Jack. "The boat!"

His dad reached out wordlessly and took the boy under his arm, shaking his head as the thumping sound of a Coast Guard helicopter's blades broke the silence overhead.

Fire.

Sirens.

Sinking . . .

The cinnamon buns were a little crispy but not burnt, and thank goodness we had them: everyone needed some sugar to help with the shock. Piper had poured extra-thick layers of the creamy sugar frosting over them, so they were sticky and almost too sweet, but much needed.

Unfortunately they did nothing to assuage my shame.

In the tiny cabin bathroom, I cried as I changed out of my wet clothes and into the cute sundress I had brought for Nantucket, which now seemed wildly inappropriate. I looked in the tiny mirror and gave myself an ultimatum: one more failure to save someone and I was quitting Junior Lifeguards. I was a menace—I did more harm than good! Pretty soon Bud would realize it and probably fire me.

I took a deep, shuddering breath in through my nose, dried my eyes, squared my shoulders, and prepared myself to go out and thank Samantha for finishing what I had started in the water. I was sick with humiliation from having to do it. I hate to fail. It feels like losing, which I hate even more. And I knew it was selfish but I really hated that Samantha had come out the winner.

Out in the cabin, Piper looked me up and down and wordlessly took off her fleece and handed it to me. I nodded my thanks, not trusting my voice just then, and pulled the fleece on over my head. Then she offered me the plate of cinnamon buns, which had been cut into quarters for easy eating. I took a quarter and placed it in my mouth, suddenly starving.

Glancing around, I could see that my dad had given Michael the dry sweatshirt and sweatpants that he keeps on board for sudden weather changes. Somehow Michael's leg was in a position that looked normal again, but the kitchen towel his mom now held against the cut on his head had become saturated with blood.

"Thank you so much," Helen said to me. "What's your name, sweetheart?"

"I'm Jenna," I said sheepishly. *The one who almost let your son drown*, I wanted to add, but I didn't.

"Jenna, I'm Helen Kim and this is Michael. Honestly, you were so brave back there, jumping in the water like that. I don't know what we were all thinking, just standing there." She stared off into space, lost in her daydream. I think she was in shock. Piper offered her another cinnamon bun but she declined it.

"Yeah, well . . . we're all Junior Lifeguards," I said, gesturing to Piper and Ziggy, and then outside to wherever Selena and Samantha were.

Where *was* Samantha, anyway? I'd expected her to be in here, in the cabin, shaking and swaddled in towels, recounting her own heroics, but she was nowhere to be seen. It was actually fine with me, since I had no idea what to say to her. *Thanks for saving my victim? Thanks for showing me up?* Obviously I was happy that Michael had been saved; I just wished I'd been the one to do it. I was sure I would have had him on the boat in seconds if I'd been left to do it on my own. Wouldn't I have?

"Junior Lifeguards! How useful . . ." She was distracted again, blotting Michael's head, so I took a deep breath and left the cabin to find Samantha.

Outside, my dad was on the radio with the Coast Guard getting updates on the *Free Spirit* and giving updates on our passengers. A fireboat was coming out from the harbor to deal with the *Free Spirit* wreckage, and they were telling us to pull into the Chatham dock, where an ambulance would meet the *Free Spirit* family.

I looked to my right and there was Samantha, loosely draped in a small towel over her bikini, tending to a cut on Mr. Kim, the *Free Spirit* dad's, hand. My heart sank even further. What *was* this girl, some kind of superhuman combination of Florence Nightingale and Wonder Woman?

I stood in the doorway of the cabin looking out as Samantha carefully bandaged the man's hand. She didn't even notice me, not that I was particularly worth noticing right now. I felt useless and hopeless.

Mr. Kim was talking to my dad and I listened as he related the events of the fire.

"We chartered the *Free Spirit* from Chatham Skipper for the day," said Mr. Hammon. "We were going to take her over to Nantucket and Tuckernuck to see some friends. We're visiting from Virginia and we have a boat down there, so we do know what we're doing. It was just the combination of the fog, and then that shoal—I had no idea—and when we hit, something popped inside the console, and there were sparks, and . . . it all just escalated so fast."

My dad was shaking his head. "Something's off about that boat. That shouldn't happen. And the radar should have warned you off that shoal."

Mr. Kim shuddered. "I can't thank you enough, honestly. What would we have done if you hadn't come?" A sob escaped his throat and he coughed to mask it.

My dad graciously looked away. "Don't think about it. You'll drive yourself crazy. I'm just glad we were out there. It's a quiet day, not that many boats out, and with everyone diverted to the ferry grounding off the Vineyard, well . . . it was just a series of bad events."

The man nodded, then he realized Samantha had finished her nursing work on him. "Oh, honey, thank you so much for that and most of all for saving Michael. What's your name?"

"Samantha," she said, extending her left hand to shake, since his right hand was injured. They both kind of laughed. "And that's Selena."

Selena nodded and said hi.

Then they all noticed me. I wanted to die.

"Jenna! Hey. You're okay!" said Samantha, all generous and concerned. I couldn't tell if she was pretending or for real.

Like, why wouldn't I be okay? I wanted to say.

"Yeah." I shrugged. "Aren't you cold?" I asked.

I couldn't help it. I didn't mean to be accusatory, but I felt jealous and spiteful, like she'd stolen my save. It wasn't as if Michael had been about to drown out there; I would've gotten him in sooner or later. *Wouldn't I have?*

She shrugged. "I think the shock of it all was keeping me warm, but now I'm going to go inside and get cleaned up. Nice work out there," she said.

I stepped aside to let her into the cabin. "Yup. You, too." But why had she been able to get Michael to move and I hadn't?

"Young lady, what's *your* name?" asked the other dad.

I introduced myself and he told me his name was Jack Kim.

"Your girl?" he asked my dad, and my dad nodded.

"Only one I've got," he said. "Three boys back home, though."

"You're one brave young lady, diving into the water like you did back there, throwing caution to the wind for someone else's sake."

I laughed awkwardly. "It wasn't my finest hour," I said, somehow echoing the movie title from the Coast Guard presentation the other day. "I didn't get him out."

"Hey, listen, he got out and that's what matters. We were all paralyzed and your jumping in was incredible. I should have done it myself. I'm going to have nightmares for the rest of my life about that."

"Oh, I hope not," I said awkwardly. He probably would, though. "Anyway, we're all training to be lifeguards, so it's like, par for the course."

He continued. "Well, they're doing a great job teaching you. But you can't teach courage, and you have that in spades, young lady."

I ducked my head in embarrassment. "Thanks." *But courage didn't get the job done*, I thought.

"You should be real proud of her," he said to my father.

"Oh, we are," my dad replied, winking at me.

Well, I'm *not proud of me right now!* I wanted to shout.

I excused myself and dipped into the cabin to check on everyone there. Selena followed me, putting her hand on my shoulder and squeezing warmly as we walked. I figured it meant she understood how I was feeling. Inside the cabin, she snagged a slice of cinnamon bun and waved to Ziggy to go back outside with her.

Samantha was now dressed and handing a mug of hot tea for Michael to his mom to help him drink it. Jack and Freddy were nestled in on the daybed beside Michael, and they seemed to be doing a little better than he was—Piper had them playing games on her phone and they were giggling quietly.

Mrs. Kim, Helen, was a wreck, especially about me and Samantha.

"I simply cannot believe you girls dove in the water to save our Michael. I actually can't *believe* it. I can never thank you enough. It should have been me going in after him. I just froze." Tears leaked from the corners of her eyes.

"It's okay, really. I'm a Junior Lifeguard. I've trained for this sort of thing," Samantha was saying.

It wasn't totally true—we'd never trained for an open water rescue, though we had the basics in place. But more importantly, why hadn't she said "*We're* Junior Lifeguards, *we've* trained"?

"Thank you," croaked Michael, looking back and forth between me and Sam. He really was so handsome. He had thick black hair that swooped back from his forehead, and his strong dark eyebrows slashed across his brow and angled a little up at the ends in a dashing way. But all the darkness was complemented by his bright white, straight teeth and dimples. I wished I'd saved him all by myself. It would have been so romantic. I could just see us telling our grandchildren the story one day . . .

"No problem. Anytime," I said. "I mean, not that it's going to happen again."

"Sorry you were in there so long," said Samantha, shaking her head ruefully.

Was that a dig against me? It sure sounded like one. I looked closely at Sam. It could be hard to tell if she was being careless or intentionally cutting sometimes.

"I might be a rescue swimmer with the Coast Guard when I'm older." continued Sam.

"What?" I spluttered. "*How?*"

Samantha smiled at me indulgently. "Kristen said there are ways to enroll, even if I'm not a citizen yet."

OMG. I wished I could just go home and be alone right now. I left the cabin again to just get away from Samantha and see how close we were to land.

Ziggy and Selena were back outside on deck. Selena had her phone and Ziggy was filming her telling about the boat fire for Facebook Live. She pressed stop when I reached her.

"That was crazy!" I said in a low voice.

"So scary," said Selena with a dramatic shiver.

"You are so brave, Jenna!" said Ziggy, eyes wide.

I scoffed. "Not really."

Selena's jaw dropped. "What do you mean, 'not really'? No one but you jumped in when that kid fell!"

"Well, Sam did," I said darkly.

"*After* you did!" Selena said.

"Hmm. I wish she hadn't."

"Why?" asked Ziggy, surprised. "You obviously needed two people to get him out. He had a broken leg and he was disoriented."

That wasn't how I saw it. "Well, *she* really got him out," I said.

"I'd say you both did, dude," said Ziggy, shaking her head.

"Does it really matter? Thank God he made it. You were both brave to get in there to fish him out! *Dios mio!*" said Selena.

We were all quiet for a minute.

"I think we'll have to reschedule Nantucket, unfortunately," I said quietly.

"Oh, please, we totally understand. I don't think any of us feels too shoppy, or whatever, right now," said Ziggy.

"Yes, I am not feeling very nacho-y right now," said Selena with a grin.

I glanced at her phone. "Did you get footage of the accident?"

Selena shrugged—I think she assumed I would be annoyed, but I wasn't.

"I don't mind, I was just curious," I explained.

Selena looked down at her screen and tapped it a few times. "I got this, but I'm not going to post it." She pressed play and a video of Michael falling in the water and me jumping in after him danced across the screen. A few seconds later there was another splash as Sam followed us in. Then the video ended.

"Yikes!" I said.

She looked at me solemnly. "And this . . ."

It was a shot of us pulling away from the *Free Spirit* and right then—*Pop!*—the boat burst into flames.

"Wow. Gosh, Selena. That's major."

"I know," she said quietly. "I don't know if I should delete it or what."

"I wouldn't delete it, at least for now. Just don't post it on Facebook, okay?"

She swatted me. "As *if*! Seriously, *chica*?"

"Sorry." I shrugged. It wouldn't be right to post

someone else's near-tragedy online, but it had been kind of cool to see myself going in for the save. I only wished . . .

I sighed, and looked out over the water. "Fog's lifting."

Ziggy nodded. "It's supposed to be beautiful tomorrow."

Selena tapped on her phone and pulled up the weather. "High of eighty, not a cloud in the sky."

"Nice," I said.

We were passing more and more boats now, which meant we were nearly at the mouth of the harbor.

Suddenly I heard a police siren, loudly blaring. I turned to see where it was coming from and spied a Coast Guard boat, just like the ones we'd visited the other day at the pier, roaring up behind us.

"Oh, we've got an escort!" called my dad in a chipper voice. "That was the least they could do!"

The Coast Guard boat raced past us and pulled just ahead of us; as they passed, the officers waved us on to follow them, so my dad—rather than taking the boat down really slow as we reached the harbor—kept it at full-throttle all the way in.

Every person on every boat we passed in the channel turned to stare at us. We must've been quite a sight: the Coast Guard motorboat racing along, being chased by a lumbering full-sized fishing boat at full speed. Our wake left tiny boats nearly swamped behind us, but I had to laugh. It was fun!

We reached the pier in record time from the Chatham bar and there was an ambulance pulled all the way down to the tie-up, where cars aren't even allowed to go. The EMTs had wheeled a gurney down to the edge of the pier, and stood there waiting for us.

My dad cut the engine and did a drift in to the side of the dock.

"Nice driving, cowboy!" said a Coast Guard officer as their boat pulled up next to ours. My dad just grinned. "We're gonna need you all to file a report."

My dad saluted at the Coast Guard guy and set about tying up our boat and off-loading the Kim family. The Coast Guard boat went off to tie up down by their berths.

Mr. Kim hopped right off to speak to the EMTs about Michael's injuries. Mrs. Kim came out of the cabin with Michael leaning heavily on her, hopping on one foot, the dishcloth pressed to his head. The two brothers, Jack and Freddy, followed.

When the small group reached me and my dad, Mrs. Kim inched Michael's arm off her shoulder and over Jack's and she grabbed my dad and then me in huge bear hugs. She was sobbing now and couldn't even speak.

"It's okay, I know. It's okay," said my dad soothingly. "It's all over. Shhh. Don't worry."

She nodded and blew us all a teary kiss and then helped the EMTs get the boys off the boat. Once they were off, Mr. Kim came back to shake all of our hands and thank us again.

"Go! Go! We'll stop by the Medical Center in a bit to see if you need anything, okay?" said my dad.

Mr. Kim pressed his lips together firmly and

nodded one short nod; I could tell how grateful he was.

As the ambulance roared away to the Cape Cod Medical Center, the six of us just stood there and looked at each other for a moment.

"Wow," said Piper finally, shaking her head.

"That was crazy," agreed Ziggy.

Now that all the adrenaline had worn off, we were all having a major energy crash. I think we were in shock, too.

"Girls, I'm so impressed," said my dad, shaking his head. "You all were dynamite out there. Thank goodness there were so many of you! We needed all hands!"

"Speaking of which, should we off-load the fish?" asked Samantha.

My dad laughed and pointed at her. "'Atta girl!" he said. "I like the way you're always thinking about the fish!" We all laughed.

"Hello!" called a woman's voice from up on the dock. We turned. It was Kristen, the Coast Guard from the other day.

"Hey!" we all called back and waved to her.

"Oh, hey Junior Lifeguards!" she laughed. "Permission to board?"

"Come on down," said my dad, gallantly offering her a hand.

She and my dad introduced themselves and then she said, "I've got to go chase after that family to the Medical Center. I just wanted to check and see if you're all okay?"

"Thanks," said my dad. "We're fine. These two jumped in the water to save one of the kids"—he pointed at me and Samantha, and Kristen's eyes grew wide—"but it all turned out okay."

"Wow, girls! I'm impressed! Do you think you might have some time to give me a statement when you're all finished here? I have to do an Incident Investigation Report."

My dad was nodding; he knew why she was here. "Absolutely. We were thinking to grab some lunch for the family and bring it up to the Medical Center. Should we just meet you there?"

"Perfect. Thanks," said Kristen as she climbed back off the boat.

"I have some videos!" piped Selena. "Of the rescue. And the boat on fire."

Everyone was quiet; Kristen turned to look at her, her eyebrows high. "Great! Can you send them to me, please?" She shared her email address with Selena and went off on her way.

"All right, let's unload these fish. I'll cut them up and filet them and you girls can take them home for dinner. Great work. And sorry about Nantucket . . ." said my dad.

All the girls clamored to tell him they didn't mind, it was no problem, what an exciting day they'd had anyway, and so forth, but my dad put his hands in the air to quiet the hubbub.

"I'll take you all tomorrow. Beautiful weather in store, no fishing on the way, ten AM departure. Okay?"

They started to protest, but he wouldn't hear it. "It's done!" he said.

I squeezed him in a sideways hug. "Thanks, Daddy," I said, using my baby name for him.

"You kids deserve it," he said gruffly. Then he opened the hatch and started hauling out the fish.

We hadn't been there five minutes before Picky Sid came strolling along.

"Hello, Bowers," he said to my dad.

My dad nodded once. "Sid."

The girls were confused; my dad was usually really friendly. Why was he being so cold to this guy? They stopped what they were doing—Selena packing up the breakfast food, Ziggy doing dishes and neatening up the cabin, Piper and Samantha stowing the life preserver and ropes and other gear—and looked up at Sid, then back at my dad. The tension in the air was thick.

"How was the haul today?" asked Sid.

My dad rolled his eyes. "I took the kids out, Sid. Not a big day."

"Good. Then it won't take me too long to check," said Sid, jumping from the dock down onto our deck.

My dad dropped the fish he was working on and it landed with a splat on the deck. My friends kind of jumped in surprise, and my dad took a step back and folded his arms to wait.

Picky Sid pulled out his little tape measure and pocket scale and began measuring and weighing the fish while my dad stood by, sighing loudly. He pulled the other fish out of the hold and worked his way through them, too. By the time he got to the fifth of the six fish, Sid did a little hiss of air in through his teeth and started shaking his head. "A little small, this one." He was acting regretful, like he was sorry to be the bearer of bad news, but we all could tell he was relishing it.

My friends and I looked at each other. Fishermen could be fined or even lose their commercial permits and licenses if they broke restrictions on fishing dates or catch limit or size limits. Fishing regulations were no joke.

My dad peered over Sid's shoulder. "Black sea bass? Looks legal sized to me."

Sid pulled his measuring tape again and measured from the nose of the fish to the end of its body, where its tail began. He looked up at my dad. "Eleven inches."

My dad sighed heavily. "Sid, you're really gonna

hassle me on one inch on a fish I took with a bunch of kids? You really have it in for—"

"Excuse me?"

Everyone turned around. It was Ziggy. "Sorry to interrupt, but the updated fishing regulations as of April eighteenth say that black sea bass should be measured from their nose or jaw all the way to the tip of their tail."

Sid stared blankly at Ziggy. My dad looked confused.

Ziggy shrugged. "They updated the regulations. Do you mind showing us how you're measuring it again, please?" She was being super-polite but Sid was quietly furious. He shot a look at my dad and my dad shrugged. The Sid gave an aggravated sigh and remeasured the fish.

"Fifteen inches," he said, glaring at Ziggy.

"Thanks," said Ziggy. She popped back into the cabin.

No one said anything as Picky Sid measured the final fish and found it legal. He stood, leaving the fish all over the deck where he'd tossed them. He shook his finger at my dad. "You were lucky this time, Bowers. But I'm watching you." He climbed off the boat.

"Have a lovely day, Sidney," said my father.

When Picky Sid had gone, we all did a quiet "Whoop!" of victory and my dad ducked into the cabin to high-five Ziggy.

"How on earth did you know all that?" he asked, grinning from ear to ear.

Ziggy blushed and shrugged again. "I just did my research before I came on board." I remembered her offering to Google the PETA regulations for my dad the other day. Oh, Ziggy!

My dad mussed her hair. "Good job, kid. You take care of that motion sickness and you're hired!"

After that, my dad processed the fish quickly and bagged it for everyone. Then we hoisted our stuff off and hosed down the deck, and my dad went to tie up the boat at his berth while we waited at the truck.

"Well, that was an eventful morning, I'd say." I shook my head.

"Unbelievable," said Piper.

"I'm so glad I made it!" said Samantha.

I glanced quickly at her. Was she bragging about the save or saying she was glad she'd caught up with us on the boat?

"Why?" I asked, shaking my head in confusion. "It was awful, and we never even made it to Nantucket! Plus you had to jump in the water and save someone's life!"

Samantha smiled widely, her eyes sparkling. "But what if I'd missed the big drama and all my friends were talking about it for the rest of the summer? I'd feel so left out!"

With a shock, I realized by "all my friends" she meant us: Ziggy, Piper, Selena, and me. How could I continue to be mad about her jumping in the water to help me? How could I resent her for saving someone's life? What was wrong with me? It wasn't her fault I hadn't had a save all summer.

I reached over and gave Samantha a genuine hug. "Thank goodness you were here."

8

We off-loaded everyone at Samantha and Selena's; Selena's mom would drive Piper and Ziggy both home so we could pick up some pizza and head over to the Medical Center. My dad had called ahead so all I had to do was pop into Vinny's at the end of the Westham wharf and grab the two cheese pies and a bag of bottled waters, and then we were off.

At the Med Center, we parked and quickly found the Kims inside. Mrs. Kim was sitting with the younger boys watching TV in the waiting area, and Mr. Kim and Michael were in with the doctors.

"Hey," my dad greeted them quietly.

I held up the pizzas and the boys were out of their seats like a shot.

"Oh, you really are heaven-sent. These boys are starving and the Cheetos from the vending machines aren't cutting it. Thank you so much. How can we ever repay you?" Mrs. Kim was practically wringing her hands.

"Please. We just wanted to make sure everyone was okay. What's the news?"

"Well, Michael has a concussion and he was in shock. He got twenty-two stitches on his forehead and they're checking on the setting of his shinbone right now to make sure it didn't get jarred in the fall. Everyone else checks out just fine."

"Phew," said my dad. "Tough on that kid, though. He was a real trooper."

Mrs. Kim nodded. "This one's the trooper," she said, gesturing to me. "Where do you all do this Junior Lifeguarding training?"

I explained about Lookout Beach and Bud Slater and even mentioned swim team and how it all came about. She nodded along, listening. "Bud Slater? The man sounds like a character."

I nodded. "He is. He's really smart and he's seen it all. He's a really good teacher." *I wish I could impress him just once*, I added silently.

"Where are you all staying?" asked my dad.

"The Chatham Bars Inn," said Mrs. Kim.

"Nice!" said my dad, impressed.

"We come once a year. It's a real treat."

"Helen!" Mr. Kim was in the doorway with Kristen Healy, the Coast Guard, at his side. "Oh, hi! You're so nice to come. Oooh! Pizza!"

"Help yourselves," said my dad. "We brought it for you guys."

Mr. Kim grabbed two slices, one for him and one for Michael. "The doctor wants to see you," he said to Mrs. Kim. He handed her the slice for Michael and she stood and headed down the hall; Mr. Kim joined us for a few minutes. Kristen turned down a slice but she sat with us.

"So have you saved a lot of people this summer?" she asked me.

I shook my head. "No. No one. And I didn't even save Michael. Samantha did."

Mr. Kim looked up from his slice in surprise. "I'd say it was you who saved him. She helped at the very end, but you're the one who went in to get him. You seemed like you'd done it dozens of times before."

I shrugged. "Well, we've trained a lot."

"You were definitely well prepared."

"Mmm," I said noncommittally.

"Bud Slater does an incredible job," said Kristen. "He's great at spotting talent, too." She winked at me. "Are you guys ready to give your statements?"

Mr. Kim stayed to watch TV with his younger boys while Dad and Kristen and I went to a bench out in the parking lot where we wouldn't have to make the Kim boys overhear us and relive the accident.

Kristen asked us questions but it really just ended up with me and Dad retelling all the events of the day.

When we got to the part about Michael, though. I clammed up and let my dad tell.

"This one jumped in and saved him," he said.

But I had to correct him. "*Samantha* saved him," I said. "That's my friend," I told Kristen by way of explanation.

"But, honey, *you're* the one who went in after him."

"Yes, Dad, but *she's* the one who got him out!" I couldn't keep the exasperation out of my voice.

Kristen interrupted smoothly. "It sounds like a team effort, which is what most saves are. It's pretty rare for a lifeguard to save someone all by him or herself."

"Well, I see it that whoever pulls the person out of the water is the saver," I said, folding my arms across my chest.

Kristen smiled. "Yes, but isn't the person who keeps them from going *under* the water also the saver?"

Hmm. She kind of had me there.

"Look, the important thing is he was saved, and you are brave girls," said my dad.

"If you think of anything else, will you get in touch with me, please?" Kristen handed me her business card.

"Sure," I agreed.

Then Kristen's eyes sparkled. "And maybe you'd like to come out on a ride-along with me one time?"

My jaw dropped. "Yes! I totally would love that!"

My dad chuckled at my reaction.

"Great. Send me an email with some dates and we'll set it up, okay?" she said, standing.

"Yes, thank you so much!"

Kristen left and I sat there daydreaming for a minute, imagining myself as a Coast Guard, a rescue swimmer . . . .

"Ice cream at Buffy's?" my dad said, patting me on the head. "I think we've earned it."

"Sure, but let me see if I can say bye to Michael first, okay?"

My dad nodded. "Good call."

Inside, Mr. Kim checked and then waved us into the small curtained area where Michael was resting. He seemed tired but less stunned and out of it than he'd been on the boat, and he was definitely cute, with that dark floppy hair and eyes that sparkled, even though he was tired.

"Hey," I said quietly.

He smiled. "Thank you for saving me."

"Oh, it wasn't me . . . I—"

Mr. Kim shushed me. "Will you stop with that nonsense? You dove into deep, rough ocean water after my injured kid, and he survived. You saved him."

I smiled, embarrassed, and turned back to Michael. "I'm glad you're okay. That was a . . . memorable morning."

He nodded. "Hopefully once in a lifetime."

"If you're better next week, stop by Lookout Beach in Westham. My friends and I are always there around lunchtime. Otherwise, maybe I'll see you next year. On dry land."

We both laughed a little.

"Thanks again, Jenna," he said.

I was surprised he knew my name. "Anytime, Michael."

The "redo" of our Nantucket trip started at a much more civilized hour the next day. My friends all met us down at the pier at ten o'clock, and the day was spectacular: crystal-clear blue skies, a temperature that was already warm but not hot, and an occasional breeze. Best of all, the water was like glass.

Today we were all on time—Samantha was actually waiting at the dock when we pulled into our parking spot—and everyone was dressed in more summery clothes than the day before. We were traveling light, too, since this wasn't really a fishing outing. It was nice not to have to lug more than a cooler and a fleece down to the boat.

"Who's ready to hit Nantucket?" I cried, and we all cheered. We were extra pumped after our failed journey yesterday, plus it turned out that this would be far nicer weather for shopping and wandering the town.

We all helped my dad get the boat ready for departure and then we were under way, the cool breeze lifting our hair from the back of our warm necks and Selena's playlist on the stereo.

"This is so much better than yesterday!" said Ziggy. "I don't even feel sick!"

"Don't speak too soon, sister. We're still in the harbor." But I wasn't actually worried. With the calm seas and the direct trip today, there was little chance of nausea for Ziggy.

"I've got a whole list of all the places I want to take you!" said Samantha.

I felt the familiar annoyance flare inside me but I pushed it down. Nothing would ruin this day for me. We'd earned a great time.

My dad let everyone take turns at the wheel, and he pointed out other boats he knew on the way, explaining who owned them and what they used them for. Even I was surprised by how well he knew the waters and the people on them.

Selena was filming again, posting directly to Facebook Live. Ziggy chatted with my dad about seabirds, Piper worked on her tan, and Samantha asked us all about our summer jobs (she was the only one who didn't have one).

The trip passed pleasantly and soon we were gliding past the Brant Point Light on our right side, Coatue on our left, and into Nantucket Harbor. As we neared the town docks, the familiar sights of distant church steeples and flapping American flags above small gray-shingled houses excited me. My dad had secured a berth at the Nantucket Boat Basin for the day through his connections, which put us right at the center of the action in town.

We clambered off the boat onto the dock and waved goodbye to my dad. We made a plan to meet at Vineyard Vines on Straight Wharf in an hour to head out to Millie's for lunch, then we headed up Commercial Street to cut over to the shops on Main Street.

"All right, what should we hit first?" I asked,

consulting the list I'd made and reading out the shop names.

"Ooh, I love the Roberta Roller Rabbit stuff at Erica Wilson!" said Samantha, consulting my list. "We always stop by Roberta's stores when we're in the Hamptons! She does great beach cover-ups and the best necklaces, and Erica's daughter Vanessa is a doll!"

"Okay . . ." *Here we go*, I thought. *Do I hand over control of the day to Samantha or do I fight her every step of the way?*

"And Monelle! I was there last season. They have the most darling gold sandals from my favorite cobbler in Capri!"

Selena and I exchanged a look, and I handed Samantha my list to add to hers.

"Lead the way," I said, shrugging. I just wanted to have a good day. I took a deep breath and tried to be Ziggy-like and zen about Sam taking over.

Samantha chattered on, playing tour guide, as we walked. Piper listened politely and Selena locked in as soon as Sam started mentioning celebrities she'd seen there. Ziggy was marching to her own drummer as usual—smiling at babies in carriages and spotting juice bars and macramé plant holders.

"Back there is Cru, where we always stop for Oysters when the Krafts' yacht drops us off."

"Do you mean the family who own the Patriots?" said Selena, wide-eyed.

Samantha laughed breezily. "Oh is that the American football club they own? I can never remember the name! Yes. My parents let me try champagne last time we were there."

"Wow!" said Piper.

"Yuck," said Ziggy under her breath. I grinned.

"Over a block is The Pearl. We had the most amazing salt-and-pepper lobster cooked in a wok. We sat with Mario Batali and Gwynnie; they are such a hoot together! Have you seen their cooking show?"

Selena was eating it up and Piper looked interested, but Ziggy was rolling her eyes and making throw-up faces at me behind Samantha's back. I felt bad but it made me feel better.

"Ooh! Here's Monelle! Our first stop, right on the corner!" said Samantha.

We stepped up into a beautiful women's boutique and everywhere I looked were colorful, appealing things. Sheer beach cover-ups and smart little party dresses, and baskets and baskets of sandals: just what I needed!

"Look at these earrings!" said Selena, holding a pair of dangly pink balls up to her ears.

"Faboo!" said Samatha.

Selena looked at the price. "But they're $125."

"That's all? Let's see!" said Samantha.

A hundred and twenty-five dollars for earrings and she thinks it's a deal? I thought in surprise.

"I'm going to wait outside," said Ziggy.

"I think that's a lot," said Selena.

"But they're Rebecca de Ravenel!" protested Samantha.

"I don't care if they're Queena de Englanda, that's too much money!" said Selena.

I busied myself looking through the baskets of shoes and managed to find a cute pair of flip-flops—but they were forty-five dollars. I knew that was a good price for an upscale store like this, and I did have the money from babysitting and working at the farm stand, but I wasn't sure I wanted to part with that much cash just for flip-flops. I tried one on and looked in the mirror; the pair was attached to each other so the extra shoe dangled awkwardly when I moved or lifted my foot.

Samantha passed by, her arms laden with things.

"I'm just trying on a few frocks," she said. "Those look darling on you!"

"Thanks, but they're too pricey, I think."

Samantha squinted. "One fifteen?" she guessed.

I was shocked. "Forty-five," I corrected her.

"That's a steal! Can I see them?"

I took them off and handed the pair to her. She inspected them all over and returned the pair to me. "I think they're worth it. They're made by a good company. They'll last. I guess it's just, do you want to be able to wear them next season?"

"Like in the fall?" I was confused.

"No, like next summer."

"Oh, gosh I have no idea. My feet will probably grow by then, I think."

Sam shrugged. "I'd buy them. You never know when you'll find something cute again that fits. Will you wait for me to see what you think of these outfits?"

"Uh . . . sure?" I said. I was eager to keep moving since we only had an hour and this store, while beautiful, was out of my budget range.

"I'll just be a mo'," she said, entering the dressing room.

I sighed and sat down on a small tufted bench.

"Jen?" called Piper.

"Over here!"

She appeared in front of me wearing a huge floppy beach hat that looked adorable on her. "I'm going to keep going. This stuff is awesome but it's, like, for adults. It's just too expensive." She took off the hat and put it back on a display knob.

I nodded. "I know. I'm just waiting for Samantha. She wants to see what I think of the things she's trying on."

Piper raised her eyebrows at me like, *Whaaaat?*

I raised mine back at her and shrugged, palms in the air, like, *What can I do?*

Selena came over. "Let's hit it. This stuff is too expensive."

"I'm just waiting for Sam. She'll just be a 'mo'!" I wiggled my eyebrows mischievously.

Selena got it. "Okay. Meet us up the block. We'll text you if we cross the street."

"Got it." I sighed and waited for Samantha to come out. After another minute I called, "Sam?"

"Ta-da!" She burst out of the dressing room in a floor-length sheer pink dress trimmed in gold rickrack.

"Wow! You look amazing!" I couldn't help but say. She did. "But what would you wear it for? Do you have a middle-school prom?"

Samantha laughed. "No, silly! The BANTAs, or maybe the Man Booker awards ceremony."

"O-kayyy . . . I don't know what that means but . . ."

She smiled at me. "They're black-tie affairs."

"Right. Well, if the price is right, I'd say you're done." I stood. "I'll just head after the others while you pay and you can catch up."

"No, but I've got a few more things I want your opinion on! Just wait. I'll be back in a jif!"

Sighing, I sat back down and looked at my watch. Fourteen minutes of our allotted shopping hour already spent in a store where I couldn't afford anything.

A few minutes later, Sam reappeared in a yellow sundress with cute blue straps and her hands in the pockets, twirling.

"Pretty!" I said, standing. "Another winner. Honestly, Sam, you look great in everything. You could be a model."

Samantha scoffed. "My parents won't let me. The agents beg me when I'm at the fashion shows but Mummy always says no. She's lived that life and she says it's grueling and unhealthy and she wouldn't wish it on her worst enemy."

"Oh. Well. It must be nice to know you're wanted," I said lamely. "Are you all set now?"

Samantha laughed. "You just don't like shopping, do you, missy? Stay put. I'll be right back!"

I wanted to tell her that I like shopping when I can participate, but that would have sounded rude. I looked at my watch. Twenty minutes gone by. I'd stay for one more dress and that was it.

Sam burst out of the dressing room in a gold bikini next and I wanted to jump up and cover her with a towel.

As much as I wanted to extricate myself from this, I had to speak out. "No way!" I said. "Way too old. Not appropriate."

"Oh, but I think it's cute!" she said, preening in the mirror. A young man shopping with his girlfriend nearly tripped over a basket of flip flops, he was so agog at Sam's outfit. I bustled her back into the changing room with a firm "No!"

Twenty-five minutes had passed and my annoyance finally beat out my manners.

"Sam, I'm heading out. Call me when you're done here and we'll meet, okay?"

"Oh, Jenna, please? Just one more?"

I felt bad but I had to stand firm. This was totally unfun.

"Nope. See you soon," I said, and I fled the store in relief.

Now, where were my real friends?

It took a few minutes to catch up to the others but they were in a much more appropriate store up the block called Stephanie's. Selena was trying on a cute denim romper and Piper had chosen a pair of printed shorts she liked. Ziggy was playing with a cat outside.

"People, what I just lived through back there was insane," I said, flipping through the racks of cover-ups. "That girl has no sense of budget and she's totally self-absorbed. She just wanted to try on outfit after outfit while I sat there like a one-girl audience. It was so boring!"

Piper shook her head. "She lives in a bubble. A one-percenter bubble."

"My mom says she's lonely," said Selena, making a face like she didn't agree. "Maybe she misses her real friends."

"Well, is that what she does with her 'real' friends back home?" I asked rhetorically. "Spend money all day long and admire each other's purchases?"

"Maybe they're all richies, too," said Piper. "Maybe that's what richies do. Spend, spend, spend!"

"If she buys even one of those outfits . . ." I said, shaking my head. I sighed. There was nothing for me here either. I always put things to the test my mom gave me: *Want or Need?* Things are rarely "needs" and I couldn't afford "wants."

My friends quickly made their purchases and we left. We still had about twenty-four minutes. We stood in a shady patch of sidewalk and debated what to do next.

"I wish I could see everything these stores had, from, like a bird's-eye view, and then we could decide . . ." said Piper.

"Yeah," agreed Selena. "Like if we had a crystal ball . . ."

"OMG!" I said. "We still haven't discussed . . ."

"Ziggy's predictions!" cried Selena, her eyes wide. She clapped her hand over her mouth and shook her head from side to side.

Ziggy shrugged and giggled. "Yeah. That was weird!"

"Weird?" I knocked her with my elbow. "You're psychic!"

Piper raised her eyebrows. "I just can't believe it, really. How did you know?"

Ziggy laughed again. "I *didn't* know! It just . . . came out of me!"

We started walking as we chatted. "I hope you're right about me and the man and the pearls and my acting success," said Selena.

"And me and my cute big guy with animals on an island!" added Piper.

"I wish you'd do a new one for me," I said.

Ziggy squeezed me in a hug. "Maybe. I'm scared to see what might come out next time, though!"

We crossed the street and headed down the other side. There were fewer interesting stores but we did pop into Erica Wilson where they had those Roberta things Samantha was talking about.

"Oh, these are the cover-ups Sam was mentioning," I said. We all gathered to look at them.

Just then the door jingled and Sam strolled in, her arms laden with bags from Monelle.

"There you girls are!" she trilled across the store.

We collectively cringed. Between the outfit she was wearing, the gold sunglasses on her head, the long dangly earrings, and the arms full of bags, she was just the kind of awful tourist you'd want to avoid.

"Yoo-hoo!" she called again, cutting through the displays to reach us.

A voice called out, "Samantha? Samantha Frankel?"

Sam spun and squealed. It was the store founder's daughter, coming over to give Sam big kisses and ask after her family.

Oh.

Sam introduced us all and the woman beamed at us, saying how lucky we were to be friends with such a "lovely young lady." We all smiled and nodded and then she left us to shop.

The things were very pretty but a little pricey for our budget, so we reluctantly left. Sam stayed behind in the store for a couple of minutes chatting with the owner as we began a slow stroll back to our meeting point to find my dad and Rory and head over to Madaket for lunch.

Samantha was breathless as she caught up to us, her shopping bags flapping.

"Would you like help with those?" asked Piper. She was always such a sweetie. Even if I'd thought to help Samantha, I wouldn't have offered, just on principle. I mean, people shouldn't buy more than they can carry, especially at our age!

"Actually, I have a few things for you girls! A few gifties for my Cape Cod besties!"

We all looked at each other. *What?*

Sam began handing around the bags—one for each of us.

I peered inside mine: the flip-flops.

Selena lifted out the pink dangle earrings, and Piper the big floppy hat. Ziggy extracted a tie-dyed scarf she'd admired in the window outside Monelle's, and we were all speechless for a second. Sam had just spent a fortune on us!

"Samantha! We can't accept these gifts! It's too much!" I spoke first and all the others quickly agreed with me, attempting to replace the items in the bags and hand them back to Sam.

But Samantha was having none of it. "I adore giving gifts and I'm quite good at it. Now, accept them and wear them with pleasure. I insist!"

When it became clear there was no alternative, we each gratefully accepted our gift and thanked Samantha profusely.

"You are one crazy lady," said Ziggy, shaking her head.

"I love it! I love Nantucket! I love you guys!" Samantha was on a shopping high, it seemed. We walked back toward Straight Wharf; I hoped to pop into Vineyard Vines at the end of the street.

Up ahead was a small gaggle of people on the sidewalk. They were peering into an upscale store window and everyone seemed very excited. We slowed down as we passed and the noise from the crowd grew.

"Here she comes! Here she comes!"

Selena could smell a celebrity a mile away.

"Who is it?" she asked a bystander.

"Queen Cee!"

"OMG, what???" Selena craned her neck to look inside, while simultaneously hyperventilating and fanning herself with her hand. "OMG, OMG, OMG!" she kept chanting.

"Celeste? The most famous singer in the world, married to the rap mogul billionaire Kay-V?" I asked.

The lady nodded.

We stopped and sure enough, the world's biggest music star exited the store and began crossing the pavement to a waiting vintage convertible Jeep. But suddenly she stopped and looked right at us. My heart was in my throat.

"Sammy?" she said.

"Cee!" cried Samantha.

The two rushed together and embraced, chattering all the while, asking after each other's families, smiling, and admiring each other's outfits.

My friends and I actually had our jaws on the floor. Samantha quickly pulled us over and we each got to meet her, and Sam took a quick selfie of us all with her (Selena chanting, "OMG, OMG, OMG," the whole time). But the crowd had grown insane and the Queen was late for her next appointment (lunch on the yacht!) and she had to dash. With lots of kisses and well-wishes for each other's family, the two reluctantly parted.

People were staring admiringly at Samantha after Cee left, but she didn't seem to notice. She just picked up her bags and kept walking, and we all scurried to catch up.

"Um, Sam? What the heck?" I said. "You know Celeste?" It was stating the obvious but what else could I say?

Samantha laughed. "Oh, we were stuck together in a hotel in Cap Ferrat during the mistral on season, and we played endless rounds of Parcheesi while we waited out the storm. She and my parents are friends. She's lovely."

Selena couldn't even speak now, she was so undone by the encounter, and Piper was actually teary.

"I just met Celeste!" she kept repeating, as if in a trance.

"Who was that lady again?" asked Ziggy, and I swatted her on behalf of everyone.

"Seriously, Ziggy? Are you for real?"

I guess Samantha had been telling us all along that she led a glamorous life, but it can be hard to tell sometimes what was bragging or fantasy and what was reality. I realized today that actually, none of it was bragging or fantasy. It was probably all real; everything she'd ever mentioned that sounded like a fairy tale was true.

I had to rethink my entire opinion of her, and it wouldn't happen in an instant.

Up ahead my dad was leaning against a big blue Suburban. He waved and his cousin Rory leaned out of the driver's side window and waved, too. We jogged up to tell them what had happened and once in the truck, regaled them all the way to Madaket with our stories.

The nachos were as good as I remembered. Strong chips, smothered in cheddar, topped with dollops of creamy guacamole and sour cream, and sprinkled with black beans, onions, tomatoes, and jalapenos. *Amazing!*

We got two orders and then everyone ordered tacos and Cokes and we chowed down. Sitting upstairs, we had a 360-degree view of the ocean and with the clear weather, we could see for miles. The breakers were rolling in onshore, but there were lots of people on the beach enjoying the day. There was a really cute African American guy with long dreadlocks at the next table; he was about our age and Piper could not stop sneaking glances at him and smiling. He had on a T-shirt from a Nantucket horse farm, which made us all giggle and nudge Piper even more. But despite our teasing her that he was the guy from Ziggy's prediction, Piper was too shy to do anything about it.

After we finished eating, my dad and Rory chatted with some friends at the next table, and we begged off to go down to the ocean. We'd get ice cream back in town before we got on the boat to go home.

We crossed the parking lot and entered the cut through the dunes and onto the warm, soft sand.

"I love it here!" squealed Selena, flinging her arms in the air. "Soft sand, no rocks, celebrities, fish tacos, expensive clothes! This is the life for me!"

Ziggy was busy looking for signs of plover birds, and Piper was looking for more cute boys. Samantha seemed happy and kind of at peace—no need to brag or storytell; what we'd just seen in town validated everything she'd ever told us. We walked toward the water, the last forty yards so burning-hot under our feet that we had to jog the last bit, shouting and hot-footing it with our knees high in the air. By the time we got to the water's edge we were screaming. I could practically feel my feet hiss as they hit the water.

The waves were bigger than they'd looked from upstairs at Millie's and there was a ton of foamy whitewater churning in front of the break.

"A little wild," said Piper. She looked around. "No lifeguards here?"

I glanced around and spied a tower way down to my left. "Further down, it looks like."

I heard a shriek to my right and saw that Samantha had thrown off her sundress to reveal a blue sparkly bikini and was plunging ahead into the water.

"Sam! No! We're leaving!" I cried, but she just waved me off and kept running into the water.

"Darn it! My dad's going to be ticked," I said.

"And we don't have a towel for her," said Piper, folding her arms.

Ziggy squinted. "Is she okay out there?"

"She's a great swimmer. Probably the best of us. I mean, nothing personal, Jenna. But probably the best ocean swimmer."

"Yeah, well, when your whole life's a vacation . . ." I muttered, annoyed.

But now I had to look carefully. *Was* she okay out there? Suddenly I wasn't sure.

"Umm . . . Jen?" said Piper suddenly. I could hear fear in her voice.

"That doesn't look right," said Selena. "She keeps dunking the waves but she can't seem to get up for enough air in between. They're coming too fast!"

"Aaargh! Why did she have to do this?" I ripped off my sundress and dashed into the water. "Get a lifeguard!" I called over my shoulder as I ran.

I saw Piper sprint down the beach and Ziggy run back to the restaurant and Selena begin filming on her phone. And I dove into the bracing water, catching my breath as I ducked repeatedly under the small but strong whitewater waves.

I did a butterfly stroke out to where I'd last seen Samantha, then I stopped and looked around. I could still stand here but I couldn't see much past the breakers rolling in.

"Sam!" I screamed, turning in a small circle. "Sam!"

I looked back toward the beach and Selena was gesturing to her right. I turned to look and there was Sam, being churned by a wave. I caught sight of her hair as she rolled over the top of the wave and went under and I dove and swam to her as fast as I could.

It seemed like ages before I located her in the churn, but I managed to grab her arm and pull her away from the break.

She was shaky and coughing when we got to a slightly safer spot where we could stand. I had my arm across her back and was holding her up as she tried to catch her breath. She sagged against me and coughed and coughed. I encouraged her to walk out of the water and onto the beach.

By the time we got to the water's edge, Piper and a lifeguard were running toward us and my dad and Ziggy were running down from Millie's. Everyone converged at once and hustled us both out of the ocean and onto the sand, well away from the water. Sam couldn't talk at first as she continued to cough and even threw up a little seawater.

Piper kept patting her on the back and Rory appeared with some clean towels from his truck and wrapped us both up in them. The lifeguard questioned Selena about what had happened and Selena explained.

Finally, finally, Samantha felt strong enough to stand, and she leaned on me as we walked up the beach and out to the truck in the parking lot. Ziggy had gathered our clothes and shoes and brought them along. The tarmac was blistering, so we stopped to put on our shoes and I noted people stopping to stare at us as we shuffled to the vehicle.

One man was shaking his head. "Shouldn't allow swimming out here at all," he said to his companion.

"Oughta have more lifeguards in Madaket!" someone called.

"Are you guys okay? Do you need anything?" It was the cute boy from the restaurant. Piper grinned at him but was too overcome to speak.

"Thanks so much," I said. "We're all set." I elbowed Piper.

"Thanks," she added lamely, still grinning. He grinned back.

We bundled into the truck and my dad peppered us with questions as Rory drove. Samantha seemed to be returning to normal but my dad was shaken by the incident.

"What made you go in the water?" he kept asking.

Samantha alternated between saying, "I don't know" and "it looked like fun."

By the time we reached town, I wasn't sure if my dad was in any mood to stop for ice cream, but Rory drove directly to a new place, Jack & Charlie's, and stopped at the turn so we could all get out.

"Do you guys want to just stay in the car and we'll get you something?" asked Piper kindly, but Sam insisted on going, so I went, too.

My dad handed me money to pay for everyone and I jumped out. We walked through the patio and into the barnlike structure and perused the menu on the wall.

We placed our orders and when they came, Selena, Piper, and Ziggy went out to the patio to eat. I turned to pay at the register but Sam dove in front of me and waved a hundred-dollar bill at the cashier.

"Sam! OMG! Stop! My dad gave me money. I've got this."

"No, *I've* got this! Please, Jenna. You just saved my life. And I've got plenty to go around. Please. Allow me." She dove across the counter and waved her money at the cashier girl, who had by now put her hands in the air like "I surrender." The cashier looked back and forth between us.

Firmly, I handed the girl the money as I pressed Samantha's hand away. "I've *got* it," I said.

Samantha reluctantly pulled back, but then she commenced in trying to give *me* the hundred dollars.

"Sam, I'm paying. It's not a big deal."

"But I always pay. Everywhere. That's what I'm here for!" she said.

I stopped and looked at her. "Do you seriously think that's what you're here for?"

Samantha shrugged and looked away. "That's what I always think. And it's usually true. People invite me along so I can pay. It's not a big deal. It's what I bring to the table." She shrugged again. "We all have our strengths."

I grabbed her by the shoulder and turned her back to look at me. "Sam! We didn't bring you here to pay! Are you crazy? We brought you here . . ." I was almost going to say "because you invited yourself," but I quickly caught myself and said "because we like you. You're our *friend*."

Samantha looked unsure. "What?"

"You're our friend. That's why you're here. Not so you can impress us by spending oodles of money, or treat us to anything, or introduce us to celebrities. You're here because you're kind and you're fun and you're a great swimmer . . . usually!"

We both laughed. Was this really happening? Was I really outlining the reasons why Samantha Frankel was my friend? And did this finally *make* her my friend? I guessed so.

"Come on. We've got a boat to catch."

Back on the boat there'd been a delivery from the Erica Wilson store. Samantha had organized to buy us all cover-ups that were semi-matching. They were truly adorable and comfy and we all put them on, admonishing Samantha for yet another purchase. We made her pinky swear that there would be no more gifts this summer, then we blasted Selena's Party Playlist all the way back to the Chatham pier, screaming the lyrics to every song, especially the Celeste ones. Piper was hoarse by the time we reached shore (no pun intended) and my dad looked like he needed two Motrin. Even Ziggy had been singing along, making up lyrics when she didn't know the actual words.

At the dock, my dad tied up to let us off, and as we gathered our things and cleaned up, along came Picky Sid. We all froze.

My dad rolled his eyes and bent to continue his tasks. "No fishing today, Sid."

Picky Sid stood there until my dad looked up again. "I'm not here about the fish, Bowers. I'm not all bad, you know."

My dad raised his eyebrows as if he found that impossible to believe.

"I'm here to say congratulations. The whole

town's talking about your kid and what she did yesterday. That you?" he asked, jerking his chin toward me.

"Um, yeah? What?" Could he be talking about what had happened yesterday with Michael?

"Nice save out there in the open water. You too," he said to Samantha.

Samantha and I looked at each other like, "*Whaaaat?*"

"How do you know about me?" she asked.

"Saw the video. Impressive. Two kids. Ha! And all those grown men standing around." And with that, he walked away.

We all looked at each other.

"The *video*?" I said, turning to stare at Selena with fire in my eyes.

"Don't look at me!" she protested, backing away, palms out. "I didn't do anything with it!"

"Then how did he find out?"

Bud was the culprit, it turned out. Mr. Anti-Technology himself: the guy who always made fun of all our newfangled electronics and watching movies on our wrists and everything.

Kristen Healy had shared a snippet of Selena's video with him—the part that showed me, and then Samantha, jumping into the water after Michael Kim. And Bud had been so proud of and blown away by us, his trainees, that he'd forwarded the video to his contact at the *Cape Cod Times*, the one who usually covered the lifeguard saves.

I'd had a bunch of missed calls during the day and they turned out to be from a reporter from the

Cape Cod Times. There were also two missed calls from Kristen Healy, who felt awful that Bud had shared the video. It turned out the *Cape Cod Times* had put it right up on their website and blasted it out to their mailing list. My parents were not happy, but it was too late. They were worried Samantha's parents wouldn't be happy either, though to be honest, you couldn't tell it was either of us unless you already knew it. My dad talked the reporter into not using our names in the article or the video caption. Since we were minors, the paper had to comply. Of course everyone in town knew who it was, so when I went to get lunch on Monday before practice, three people cheered and called out to me as I rode my bike through town.

I had to admit: it felt great.

When I got to Junior Lifeguard training that day, all the other guards were standing around the pavilion, which was weird. Normally they'd all be down stretching and warming up already. It turned out there was something happening today.

Bud came out of his office door and along with

him were the Kims! They came to us out on the deck and Mrs. Kim hugged me and Samantha. She looked a lot better than she had the other day.

Bud whistled and stood up on a chair to talk to us.

"Gang! This is the Kim family. They're the ones the Bowers crew helped out at sea on Saturday. You may or may not have heard the story about their rental boat sinking and then Jenna and Samantha going into the water after one of them, but it's in the news this week and we're all awful proud of them. Let's give them three cheers right now! Come on up here, girls!"

Samantha and I looked at each other and smiled, and then joined Bud up at the front while everyone whooped and cheered. It felt as great as I'd always dreamed it would, and I knew Sam was pleased, too.

Bud high-fived us both and then quieted the crowd.

"In honor of the rescue, the Kim family has made a very kind and generous donation to the town lifeguarding program. They have endowed an annual scholarship for a town lifeguard to help supplement their college payments each year."

The crowd erupted in cheers, especially from the older guards who were dealing with college bills already. The Kims looked pleased.

Bud put his hands in the air to quiet us all down again. "And that's not all! They've also opened a tab at the Clam Pot for the rest of the summer for any Junior Lifeguards to get lunch or ice cream or anything they want, anytime, on their bill. And we will not abuse their generosity, will we, guards?" said Bud sternly.

There was another cheer, and I was smiling so hard I thought my cheeks would burst. I crossed the pavilion to the Kims and hugged each one of them, even Michael, who looked cuter than ever now that he was up and about and had a tan again. He squeezed my hand and smiled and I felt breathless for a moment. I wished he would be here for the whole summer.

I caught Hayden Jones looking at me strangely

and I smiled at him and shrugged. No harm in having him just the teensiest bit jealous, right?

Now Samantha was whispering in Bud's ear and then they both looked at me.

Bud called the crowd to attention again. "I hear there's been another save by our Miss Bowers. Yesterday, on Nantucket! You're on a roll, missy!" he said. "Let's do another three cheers for Jenna, and I know we usually wait until the end of the day, but, gentlemen . . ." He gestured to the biggest senior guards and I realized what they were going to do.

"Oh no!" I said. "You can't catch me!"

But they did, and in I went, for my first dunking. The first of many, I hoped.

It was everything I'd dreamed it would be, even though it all happened so fast. The guards—including Daniel, who was thankfully not mad at me for my spaciness the other day—scooped me up like I weighed nothing. They carried me over their heads and while I struggled a little—just as a formality—they had a firm grip on my limbs and there was no chance they were letting me go.

All too soon it was over. They tossed me and I flew through the air, landing feetfirst with a big splash in the cool water. I came up smiling and splashed them all as they turned to head back up to Bud. I could have stayed there in the water all day, soaking it in. I couldn't wait to have it happen again.

I emailed Kristen Healy that week to catch up, and also to take her up on her offer for the ride-along. We scheduled it for the following Saturday, and I had a small request that she agreed to.

That morning, my dad drove me down to the Chatham Pier and looked at me proudly across the bench seat of his Ford pickup.

"You're a chip off the old block," he said, grinning.

"You or Mom?" I asked cheekily. I knew he meant himself, but he grew thoughtful.

"Both of us, actually. You're the best of both of us. You've got my common sense and your mom's practicality. The bravery . . . well, that's all yours.

That came factory-installed." He tousled my hair. "We couldn't be more proud of you, kid."

"Thanks, Dad," I said, unbuckling and snuggling under his arm for a hug. He slowed down to park and then I spotted her and waved.

"There she is! Sam! Over here!"

Samantha was on the dock in a blue-and-white-striped long-sleeved T-shirt and white shorts with a white baseball cap and white sneakers.

I jumped out of the truck and ran to hug her. "You're looking very nautical today."

She stood up straight. "I'm going for that clean-cut, military look. How'd I do?"

I laughed and poked the brim of her hat. "You look great. Let's go!"

And we ran down the dock to where Kristen was waiting for us.

THE END

WE HOPE YOU'LL ENJOY
THIS EXCERPT FROM THE NEXT
JUNIOR LIFEGUARDS BOOK:

Take a Stand

FEATURING SELENA DIAZ!

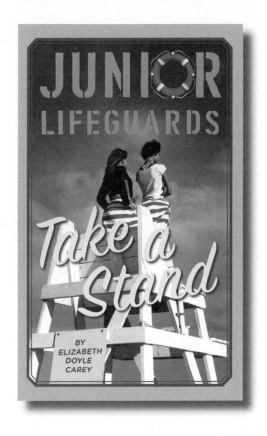

My palms tingled with nervousness as a light perspiration prickled my brow. This was *so* not in my wheelhouse, but what the heck! If this summer had taught me anything so far, it was that life was more interesting when you ventured outside of your wheelhouse. Like, *way* outside.

As an actor, I'm used to opening night jitters, and that's what this felt like—though I still had the sense that this summer I was "playing against type" (that means pretending to be a character who is very unlike the real me). And tonight would be our big performance; one I didn't want to flub.

Yes, fans, this evening's entertainment would

be the annual Junior Lifeguarding Exhibition and Family Picnic, brought to you by Bud Slater and starring the Westham Town Lifeguards. And we, the Junior Lifeguard squad, were warming up our routines for the big show.

"Okay, we've got to try this again," said Jenna, our team captain and one of my best friends, but also a relentless taskmaster.

I groaned. The late-July afternoon sun was blistering and the humid air made it hard to breathe. "Again?"

Jenna gave me a curt nod. "Just act like you're filming some superhero movie, Selena. Now get in the ready position. We go on my whistle on three. One, two…"

I am definitely more of a romantic comedy actress, for sure not an action hero, but I can act. I dropped to the sand and lay on my stomach, my forehead resting on the back of my wrists like someone in a war movie getting ready to go into battle. Then I reached deep down inside where I find my motivation for all my best roles and when Jenna blew her whistle, I tried to act like Gal Gadot in *Wonder Woman*, even though it was a real stretch. I pushed up from the sand, pivoted, and ran fifty yards to where an eighteen-inch length of garden hose stuck out of the sand. Diving for it, I clenched my hand, expecting to grasp the cool rubber but instead feeling only air as I fell. My hair fell from its messy bun and practically gagged me with its weight in my face.

Sputtering, I stood and dusted myself off. Samantha Frankel was brandishing the garden hose high in her fist. I stood there dumbly, coated head to toe in sand, like a piece of Shake 'n Bake chicken. I was no Gal Gadot in *Wonder Woman*. I wasn't even Elsie Fisher in *Eighth Grade*. I was only me: Selena Diaz, twelve-year-old landlubber lifeguard trainee, hopelessly aspiring movie star, and immigrant daughter of a maid and gardener.

I sat down heavily in the sand in frustration. Not only had I lost again, but I'd lost to my boss.

"I'm dashing home to change, loves," trilled Samantha in her fancy English accent.

"Righty-ho," I muttered. She crossed the beach to the dune path that leads right to the terrace of her beachfront estate. I usually use this path when I leave the beach, but that's only when the boss isn't in town.

Okay, so, Samantha's not exactly my boss, but her parents are my parents' bosses. My mom is the Frankels' housekeeper and my dad is their property manager, and we live in a cottage on the grounds of their estate here in Westham, Massachusetts on Cape Cod. The family is usually not here much—maybe two weeks at most—but this year, the two Frankel girls are here for the whole summer. And they're staying here in their huge estate with just a dumb male nanny named Nigel to supervise, and no parents at all.

As soon as my mom realized that Nigel wasn't proactive about anything except his own social life (he likes to go clubbing in Provincetown), she stepped in and signed up Samantha to do a summer's worth of beach activities with me at Junior Lifeguards.

Five. Afternoons. A week.

It hasn't been easy.

"Cheerio!" called Jenna after Samantha, waggling her fingers. Jenna and Sam are now kind of friends, which makes our free time outside of Junior Lifeguard training a little awkward. Like, when I ask my besties to sleep over this weekend, will I have to ask Samantha to come sleep in her caretaker's cottage? The social aspects of Junior Lifeguards have really complicated my summer.

On the other hand, doing Junior Lifeguards has been cooler than I had thought it would be. My besties Ziggy, Jenna, and Piper all do it, so we get mad quality time together every afternoon. We've had some fun adventures and I've gotten to meet two celebrities, which has been awesome.

Also, I got to meet a talent scout for the Walt Disney Company. After she heard me sing when I babysat for her kids, she gave me her business card. Honestly, I've looked at that thing so many times in the last two weeks that it's amazing it hasn't crumbled to dust in my hands.

She had asked me to send her some head-shots—professional pictures of me looking my best or showing off my skills in one way or other. The only thing is, these pictures cost a lot of money. And if I really want to do them right, I have to have my hair and makeup professionally done, too. *Ka-ching!* I have a paid summer job at the library three mornings a week, but I am not exactly rolling in the dough and neither are my parents. My mom's in grad school to become an accountant and my dad has his own landscaping business to fund. We don't have a thousand extra dollars lying around for this sort of project. We don't even have a few hundred extra.

"Alright, break time," said Jenna, reaching her hand down to hoist me up out of the sand. "Sorry you didn't win that one, but you were closer than ever!"

"I hope I do better tonight." I sighed and dusted myself off. I think the big change in me so far this summer is that I am actually willing to *try* to win a race against long-legged Sam Frankel. For a total non-athlete like me, that's saying something. And I have to admit, it's thanks to Junior Lifeguards—something I initially did not want to do at all.

"Leeny, please tell me your mom's bringing the *arepas* tonight," said my friend Ziggy Bloom. She's tiny but has a hearty appetite, even if she is a vegetarian.

"She promised!" I smiled because I love them, too.

Piper smoothed her thick blond hair into a fresh long ponytail and grinned at Jenna. "And what is the Bowers clan contributing tonight?"

Jenna Bowers's mom's family runs the biggest and most successful farm stand in the area; people travel from miles around for their homegrown organic produce and freshly caught local fish. But the highlights of the farm stand are their baked goods and prepared foods: salty, crispy fried chicken; crunchy, tart cucumber salad; creamy pesto pasta; spicy pimiento cheese dip; and chewy cinnamon buns dripping with thick frosting, to name just a few stand-outs.

Jenna laughed. "You all just use me for my food!"

Piper pretended to consider this for a moment. "Well, also for your dad's boat."

Jenna swatted her and Piper shrieked and ducked out of the way.

"Hey, girls." Hayden Jones joined us as all the kids took a break from practice. Hayden is one of the cutest guys on the Junior Lifeguarding squad. Jenna and I both kind of have a crush on him—she a little more than I—because he is very nice but also tall and fit and tan, with sun-streaked brown hair and golden brown eyes.

But Hayden's a little sketchy—he's kind of unreliable and secretive and prone to being late for things. He lives with Bud Slater, our Junior Lifeguard program director. Bud's an old family friend of the Jones family or something and he's trying to whip Hayden into better behavior since Hayden's parents are flakes and Hayden got "asked to leave" his last boarding school. I don't usually swoon over preppy guys but there's something in Hayden's combination of great looks and puppy dog sadness that make him irresistible.

"What's up, skyscraper?" I joked, since he is a good fourteen inches taller than I am.

"Want to see the weather up here?" he teased, and he suddenly knelt down, grabbed me around the knees and hoisted me way up high in the air.

"Hayden! Put me down!" I yelled, flailing, and he swooped me back down to earth. "I could see Boston from up there!" I joked as I caught my breath.

Hayden was laughing. "Now you know what it's like up here, pipsqueak!"

"I'm not a pipsqueak!" I yelled, diving at him and trying to wrestle him. But Hayden was like a sequoia tree—he didn't budge. I backed away, winded.

"You two are like those college cheerleaders on TV," said Piper, smiling. "You know, where they wear the letter sweaters in matching colors and the guy tosses the girl in the air and makes it look all easy?"

"Hmm, maybe we should have put together a routine for tonight." Hayden held his chin in his hand and tapped it with his pointer finger, like he was still considering the idea.

"As if!" I said, turning to Piper. "He'd probably drop me."

I caught a glimpse of Jenna then and realized she was not enjoying this scene a bit. Hayden was definitely a player—he flirted with all the girls—but Jenna had kind of claimed him early on. She didn't like it when she felt like I was flirting back too much. Part of me felt like, *too bad, so sad,* but Jenna was a good friend and I didn't want to hurt her. So for now, I dialed back the joking around.

"So Jen, remind me again about the timing for tonight?" I asked.

Jenna looked at her watch. "At five thirty the families arrive and set up. At six o'clock our demonstration starts. I think it should take about half an hour. After that, we eat and then have a five-minute Q&A session for kids thinking of joining the program next year!"

"And then sparklers!" said Hayden, waving his hands in the air.

"Oh, cool! Really?" said Piper.

"I have a bunch and Bud said it was okay to use them."

Leave it to Hayden to have some slightly risky doodad to enliven things, I thought.

"Be sure to pick them up when you're finished with them!" warned Ziggy. She's a volunteer on the beach cleaning crew and is always telling us how awful people are about garbage at the beach. She waved her finger at Hayden. "If I find even *one* sparkler here tomorrow…"

Hayden laughed. "Scout's Honor. I'll make sure they all get picked up."

"Hey! Were you a scout?" asked Jenna, her eyes lighting up. She loves all things even vaguely military.

"Uh, no. It's just a figure of speech," said Hayden sheepishly. I think Jenna fell a little bit out of like with him just then.

"Oh," she said, disappointed.

Suddenly one of the other Junior Lifeguards came running toward us from the parking lot. It was Summer, a girl I'm friendly with from science class.

"Hey!" said Summer. "Come check this out! There's a huge tricked-out bus in the parking lot selling lifeguarding supplies!"

There were cries of "What?" and "Cool!" and we all grabbed our flip-flops from the kick-off area by the beach fence and scampered up the hill to see what was there.

Sure enough, as I crested the dune I could see a big, flashy Greyhound-sized bus with a red-and-white photowrap over it, showing red crosses and the word *Lifeguard*, featuring photos of teen life-guards at the beach. It was awesome!

"Wow!" We hurried across the parking lot to the door of the vehicle, which was open. A short flight of steps led to the top.

We weren't sure what to do. Jenna looked at us, shrugged, then climbed the steps, calling "Hel-looooo?" She looked back at us once more but kept going.

"Helloooo?" she called as she climbed.

Then a sing-song female voice called from inside, "Hello! Come on up!"

Was it a little weird for all of us to get on some stranger's bus? Stranger danger? White van? Probably not the smartest thing. But there were a lot of us and Hayden was a big guy, so we piled up the stairs and into the vehicle.

Inside . . .

**SORRY TO END IT HERE,
DEAR READERS.**

**PLEASE BUY A COPY OF
TAKE A STAND OR CHECK IT OUT
FROM YOUR LOCAL LIBRARY, TO FIND
OUT WHAT'S INSIDE THE BUS,
AND MORE!**

ABOUT THE AUTHOR

Elizabeth Doyle Carey is a frequent visitor to the town of Cotuit on Cape Cod, where she roots for the Kettleers baseball team. Though not a lifeguard herself, she loves swimming at Dowses Beach in Osterville and stopping at Four Seas Ice Cream in Centerville for peppermint stick on a sugar cone.

Please visit

WWW.ELIZABETHDOYLECAREY.COM

to learn about other books Liz has written.

Please visit

WWW.DUNEMEREBOOKS.COM

to order your next great book or to read more

about fun stuff to do in Cape Cod

and other cool places.

DUNEMERE
Books

Do you have all of these Junior Lifeguards Books?

#1

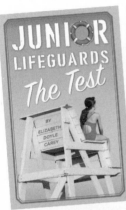

#2

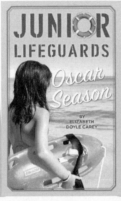

#3

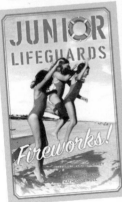

#4

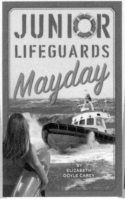

#5

#6